The War Between

T.K. Moore

D1565304

THE WAR BETWEEN

COPYRIGHT © 2022 T.K MOORE

FIRST EDITION JANUARY 2022

PRINTED IN THE UNITED STATES OF AMERICA

10 9 8 7 6 5 4 3 2 1

ISBN 9798523514784

COVER DESIGN BY STEVEN FREEMAN

Acknowledgements

Cover by Steven Freeman.

A special thanks to everyone who contributed to getting this book out there. You guys are just downright amazing!

To the readers who gave invaluable feedback: There are too many of you lovely people to list but you know who you are.

Special thanks to Nicole Travers. Without you and your support I probably would have given up at some point and cried myself to sleep.

Dear Reader,

Thank you for reading "The War Between," the First book in the *Twisted Timeline* Series.

There is One other book in this series:

• Book 2: The War Between: Twisted Timeline (not yet released)

I hope you enjoyed their story at least half as much as I enjoyed writing it! These characters have become like family to me over the past few years writing their stories.

Would you like me to write some more of them? Let me know! My email is authortkmoore@gmail.com.

If you're the Facebook type, I keep readers, fans, and anyone else up-to-date on all the latest happenings in my writing on my group page: Written In Dreams T.K. Moore

Table of Contents

Chapter 1: Struck by Tragedy

Asherah

A temple in the sky? Who would have thought?

The soft breeze blew through the open windows of my temple in the sky and brushed against my darkened skin. I sat upon my daybed, cradling a wolf pup in my arms. I smiled down at her and stroked her black fur. "Oh Cyrus, what am I going to do with you, little one?" I chuckled. Her little head tilted up at me with ears perked as her eyes stared back at me in adoration.

I poked her little nose and smiled. "You have a big job ahead of you, Cyrus. I'm going to need you to be on your best behavior. Can you do that?" I asked the six-month old pup.

Wiggling to get free of my grasp, Cyrus leapt out of my lap onto the stone floor, stretching her limbs. She turned to face me. "What do I have to do?" She mouthed.

Leaning down with the biggest smile I could muster, I explained, "Well, you're going to have to lead the other wolves down there on Earth."

A premonition played out like a movie in the back of my mind, and the screams and cries of the humans poured into my head My ears began to ring as my vision went dark.

A thickened darkness rolled in across the skies as I watched in horror at the chaos below. Those thought to be human were stripped of

1

their skin when smaller clouds of microscopic organisms chewed through their guise.

Pixies took off over their heads and rubbed their burning eyes. Their small cries fell on deaf ears. Nymphs and reptilians shifted, and their human skin fell from their shoulders. More and more bursts of lights flashed across the world, informing us in the heavens of the untimely unmasking of our star children.

The scene disappeared before me and instead I saw the silhouette of a woman. The poor thing was scared out of her wits in a room with a human I did not recognize. I narrowed my eyes at the black aura currently surrounding him. The feeling of pure undiluted evil radiated from him. Why does that man look familiar? I thought, rubbing my chin.

I shifted my gaze to the side and took another peek into the timeline and smirked. "So, it is you... you've finally come out of your shell, Seth." I watched as the God of trickery and chaos cradled a petite, white haired woman with such delicacy and care while he carried her to safety.

Pulling myself from the premonition I shook my head and chuckled. "Oh, this is going to be an interesting turn of events. Cyrus, looks like you'll be going back to Earth sooner than we thought, sweetheart.

The pup slouched her shoulders and pouted. "But I'm not big like a sphinx," she whined, pinning her ears flat.

I rose from my spot on the daybed and knelt in front of Cyrus, to cup her furry face. "My dear, you will be much bigger in due time. Now, go on—they are going to need you.

I lifted Cyrus into my arms and held her close. "You have much ahead of you sweetheart. Now go fulfill your role. Keep an eye on those two and always obey what Seth tells you." Placing the pup on a cloud, I sent her down to Earth.

I watched with tearful eyes as the cloud descended. "Until next time, little one. I'll be down shortly."

I sighed heavily before turning toward the stone table that held a pool of water in its center. Waving my hand over it, I called for Ra and a summoner named Portú. Both of their figures appeared like a watery hologram just above its surface.

Ra smiled at me with his hands folded over one another in front of him. "Asherah, to what do I owe the pleasure of your call?"

Bowing my head to him, "I need your assistance with this one. I apologize in advance if it seems completely out of the blue. But, we have quite a bit of work ahead of us. It seems we have a new problem..."

Portú hissed behind his cloak. "What does that have to do with me?"

I chuckled, shaking my head at him, "You need to prepare for the revival. Mother earth needs you more than ever."

Portú raised his hand and nodded. His water figure disappeared back into the pool before Ra decided to speak.

"Well, who is going to be included in this... endeavor?" He asked.

I sighed, "Well, for starters, I am going to need you to wake up Seth." I winced at his name.

Ra burst into a tearful laughter, "Are you sure? Is Seth the one you want? He's got another decade before he needs to stand guard. I'm not so sure he's going to be happy with you."

Pinching the bridge of my nose, I couldn't help but chuckle. "Would you rather have the earth destroyed? Or would you rather deal with Seth's temper tantrum?"

Seth

I stood staring over the pyramids. Darkness coated the sky as heavy winged machines, ones that the humans used to travel, flew overhead. I lowered my ears to escape the whooshing roar. "What is that contraption?"

"Seth, come quickly! We need to hurry!" one of my disciples called after me.

I grunted and jumped from the top of King Tut's pyramid to the burning sand, landing with ease. "What is this with which they are covering the Earth?" I sniffed the air and growled.

The chemical compound intertwined with the air caused my nose to burn. "We need to take shelter. Get everyone and go into the temple," I ordered, shifting my gaze back to the sky.

The hairs on the back of my neck stood rigid. "Something's coming. This isn't good," I mumbled to myself. I followed the others, only to seal the stone door shut as the last of my disciples had entered.

Dusk approached and my nerves sat on edge, I leapt back on top of the pyramid with ease and watched the burning orb of the setting sun disappeared beneath the sand on the horizon. My thoughts were scrambled in utter confusion while the light quickly faded. Another charge permeated the air, the warmth of the desert quickly died down.

My spirit elevated when I shifted my ear in the direction of the supposed trespasser. I inherently knew this being to be of celestial origin without having to turn around. I sat with narrowed eyes staring off into the desert.

A growl of displeasure vibrated my chest. "You woke me up a decade early for this?"

The sand covering the stone shifted beside me as the being in question stepped into my peripheral view. A dull light glowed from a flowing gown of white and gold—a goddess.

"Well, I don't think Anubis would have been able to handle this responsibility, and I've seen all I needed to see. So, what's an additional ten years on your millennia guard going to do, Seth. As you may not

4

know, the humans have launched a biochemical weapon." Her voice was sweet, yet ethereal, like my own.

I sighed. "And what is it you need from me that couldn't have waited, Asherah?" I shifted my gaze to her, and I quickly scanned over her darkened silhouette.

Asherah brought her hand to her mouth and chuckled. "Oh, you know me very well, don't you?"

"You never bring me good news, so I'm assuming this is going to be a pain in my ass and possibly a waste of my time," I replied, annoyed.

"Where did you learn such language, Seth?"

I scoffed. "The humans. Where else?"

Asherah released a long breath. "Well, back to the task at hand. They'll be hunting all of our Starseeds on Earth. You know they want all of them gone."

"And what does that have to do with me?" I growled.

"There's a girl. She will awaken once you find her. The problem is, no one knows where she is or if she's already been captured. Ra assured me her life force is here in this timeline, but he can't pinpoint her location, and neither can I. That's where you come in."

I thought for a moment, my mind swirling with the possibilities of finding a single person amongst billions in cities I had never traveled to, and which I would not like to navigate on foot. "Don't tell me. If I can't find her or if she dies, this planet is screwed." I turned back to face the desert and watched the approaching black cloud.

"That's the gist of it." She smiled and placed her hand on my shoulder. "I also have a surprise for you." Her voice faded.

A surprise? I shifted my gaze to the sand at the base of the pyramid. There sat a massive black wolf, its ears perked as it stared off into the distance. "Oh no, you're not leaving me with that thing."

Too late; already did. Take care of her. Her name is Cyrus. Oh, one more thing.

I sighed heavily, placing my head in my hands. "What?"

There's a man who wants her for himself. I don't know the reason, but from what I saw it doesn't seem good. Keep him as far away from her as possible.

"Great, so not only am I searching for this mystery child I am her babysitter too?"

She's not a child... in this timeline she's a little older than she looks.

"How long until they start changing?" I turned my head, only to find that she had disappeared as quickly as she had come. "Shit," I whispered. "Where the hell am I going to find this woman?"

Chapter 2: Rumor Has It

Ian

I was disgusted with these mythical beings on this planet. Earth wasn't supposed to be freak show. We needed pure humans and not these… freaks roaming around.

A high-pitched ringing invaded my right ear as I entered my facility. For the most part it was my research lab and torture chamber but, it was more of a prison to most of its occupants.

I stopped for a moment with my eyes shut and waited for the ringing to subside before addressing a bloodied guard

"Where are we with the griffin? Has he said anything about his counterparts or where they are hiding?" I asked.

"Sir, he hasn't said anything, but it seems his body couldn't handle the pain. He turned to stone." The guard replied.

I scoffed and continued on toward the main observation room to inspect our newest abomination.

Ceiling-to-floor screens littered the room depicting various occupants which filled the facility. Men and women hustled around the room, chatting to one another about recent events, lab results, and the conditions of our non-human guests

A clomping of double-timed footsteps approached then skidded to a stop beside me. "Sir, all weapons have been fired, and the ions have been dispersed," a soldier stated as he saluted me.

I acknowledged him with a nod, staring through the glass at the woman before me. "They'll come looking for her. You need to get her out of the facility here in Beijing. Take her back to the United States."

Her snow-white hair, cut short above her shoulders, fanned across the hospital pillow on which she lay. Her tanned skin was stained with saltwater, giving her a grayish hue. No one knew how long she'd been underwater before she had resurfaced and washed up on the shores of the Yellow Sea.

I clicked my tongue as I turned to face the elongated computerized table and checked over the stats of the others. Their heartrate monitors beeped steadily. The light overhead flickered causing my brow to arch. "What the hell was that?"

"Looks like there was a power outage across the east coast, sir," the soldier beside me responded.

I cocked my head at him and raised my brow, scanning the man from head to toe. The fine lines across his forehead matched the crow's feet that peeked from the corners of his tired eyes. "A power outage, huh?"

Shoving my hands into the pocket of my slacks, I pivoted on my heel as I spun back around to watch the mysterious woman once more. I peeked at my reflection in the glass. I had noticed lately that my own skin had become stained with a bluish hue. I shook my head, ran hand through my medium length hair, and tossed any sullen thought of my own looks aside to return my focus back to the task at hand.

This woman. What is her purpose here?

I had her DNA profile pulled and blood samples extracted to run tests to see who she was. There has been a rumor that this woman would come, but we hadn't taken any notice of it until she showed.

"Rumor has it that she's going to stop our plans. What do you want us to do?" the soldier asked.

Annoyed, I narrowed my eyes at him. "And where did you hear such rumors?"

The soldier nervously rubbed the back of his neck. "You know this place is full of those fortune tellers. I overheard one speaking of a white-haired woman and then this one shows up shortly after? This isn't a coincidence, sir.

An annoying beeping notification from the tablet in his hands piqued my interest. I peered over to see what the notification was and saw it was the woman's lab results.

"Open the file. Let's see what we're dealing with here," I ordered, crossing my arms behind my back.

My nerves were already shot when my eyes landed on her lab results. Her name remained a mystery, but her abilities involved more than just her accidentally showing up here by mistake, was she supposed to be able to jump timelines? She had the ability to wield water, harness the power of the air-- and then came the red letters I was really hoping I'd never see: "Unknown" printed across the screen under "Extended Abilities."

"Who are you? I have every one of these freaks on record but you," I whispered, bringing my hand up to stroke my chin. *How is she low on oxygen if she can breathe underwater?* I thought, releasing a long breath.

"This is going to be tougher than I thought. She needs to remain asleep until we can figure out what *all* of her abilities are. How is it that we have a slew of information on the others, but nothing that can pinpoint what the hell we're dealing with here? I slammed my fist into the glass cover of the computer system, fracturing it.

A loud, deafening emergency siren blared, causing the biochemists and scientists in the room to visibly shake in their shoes. I couldn't see the problem, as this woman was still asleep.

... Or so I thought. I kept my eyes on her chest to watch it slowly rise and fall. Her heart rate had yet to pick up. I leaned over, shifting my weight, and pressed the intercom to the secured room. "What's going on? She's still asleep."

"Sir, no, she isn't!" one cried, his voice shaking as he pressed himself against the wall. He pointed to the heartrate monitor. The slow and steady beeping began shifting into frantic, unsteady lines.

My brow arched as my gaze volleyed from her to the chemist. "What do you mean she isn't? I'm staring at her right now. She's asleep. Why is that stupid mon—" I paused.

My lips parted as water seeped between the grout of the tile floors and every available crevice within the room. Panic erupted, and everyone rushed for the doors. Protocol stated that no one was to leave the room under any circumstances if a threat emanated from within. The rising water drowned out any thought of the rule. The barrage of water quickly muffled screams, and bodies were lifted off the floor, suspended in silent death rattles, helplessly drowning as their lungs filled.

A panicked soldier ran up to me. "Sir, what do you want us to do? She's going to flood the facility!"

As quickly as it had surged, the water receded into the floor, leaving the machines inoperable and the majority of our personnel dead.

The woman slowly pushed herself up into a sitting position on the bed, rubbing the sleep from her eyes. A small moan escaped her lips as she yawned and stretched her arms to the sky. Her sapphire blue eyes slowly opened and fixated on me. "Wait... where am I?" Fear was painted across her face as she frantically searched the room for answers.

"Who are you? What the hell is all of this? Where are we?" she shouted with frightened eyes and trembling limbs. The woman quickly rose from the bed and stepped on a dead scientist. She froze as her gaze shot back up at me.

"What the fuck is all of this?" she screeched. The ground rumbled beneath our feet, the building shaking with her screams.

"Sir, we need to sedate her!" the soldier beside me shouted.

I nodded my head, my gaze never shifted, and I gave my men the signal to fire at will. Over a dozen rifles spat fire only to have their ammunition freeze in midair, then fly across the room. The bullets bounced against the tiled walls.

"Use the nerve gas and get her back under. Prep her for transport. We gotta get her out of here now!" I shouted, spinning on my heel in a desperate bid to get distance between myself and that... whatever she was.

Outside of the facility, chaos erupted. I stood paralyzed on the roof, mouth hanging open as buildings toppled from the quake this woman had caused. Those below in the streets who were unique were stripped of their human flesh, skin peeling back to reveal their true identities: wings, fur, scales, and everything in between emerging.

A burning sensation shot across my back. I reached over my shoulder sucking in a sharp breath as I pressed my hand against it. "What the hell?" I thought, bringing my hand to my face my eyes widened at the sight. My blood--only it was more purple rather than red. "Am I having a reaction to this too? Did I not think to test myself against this before I released it?" I grumbled.

I turned my gaze to the sky as human souls clouded the atmosphere. I smiled at the thought of their demise. The beginning of the new world I had wanted for so long.

And so the hunt began for the woman named Iris.

T.K. MOORE

Chapter 3: Search Party for One

Seth

I had traveled to several cities between Europe and Asia with my canine companion, Cyrus. It'd been six years, and I'd only caught the scent of this woman three times since the search began.

The first time an invisible web pulled me toward her was right after my talk with Asherah. Another flying contraption called an airplane had flown overhead, and I followed it only to watch it disappear over the horizon. From there, I traveled to what others would call the United States. We'd never traveled outside of the African continent, so the rest of the world was foreign territory.

Black smog rolled into the valleys as I sat perched on one of the surrounding mountain peaks watching the cities fall into pure mayhem. There were more mythical and spiritual beings here than I had seen in my lifetime, but with Cyrus by my side she managed to give them the sense of safety they all were searching for and guide them to the Dome.

As I stomped through the seemingly untouched brush towards an old concrete structure that looked abandoned, I could hear a female voice screaming at the top of her lungs. The ground shook, causing nearby structures, trees, and the ground to crumble. *It must be her*, I thought, feeling the invisible pull guided me through the building.

It's definitely her. That scent is familiar and the obvious vocals just like the previous times we were close enough to her. Cyrus winced, flattening her ears.

You're right. And here I thought I was the only one who could make the world shake.

Well duh, and your nose should be stronger than mine. She rolled her eyes at me.

As the wolf and I entered the building, a whooshing contraption I learned later was a helicopter took off from the top of the building and passed by a window. My gut urged me to follow after it. I growled in frustration. At that rate, I wasn't going to be able to catch up with it. Instead, I continued into the building, only to run into a horde of Soulless crowding a previously occupied room.

"What the hell?" I whispered in confusion. The walls were glass. The hospital bed in the center of the room was covered in blood. Bile rose in my stomach. I hoped it wasn't hers, fearing that I was too late. With a low growl, I pushed past the Soulless and into the room. They couldn't sense my energy, and I was grateful for that. Remnants littered the floor— bits of what looked to be men in lab coats, their skin burned to crisps.

This woman is strong... she barbecued the poor bastards. Cyrus gave me a wolfy chuckle.

How do you know it was her?

Cyrus glared at me before shifting her gaze to the strands of white hair on the floor beside the bed. *Because that has her scent all over it.*

Shaking my head, I turned to what looked to be a partially burned case file on the desk and flipped open the front of the folder. The picture was burned, and the name slot read 'Unknown.' There wasn't much information I could glean from the inside, but from the thickness of this file I could tell there was quite a bit of history and lab results listed.

"Why can't I get anything right today?" I slammed my fist into the desk, which snapped in two

THE WAR BETWEEN

Because you keep doubting your gut, Ra's voice echoed in the back of my mind.

You know this whole feeling is new to me. I don't know what the hell I'm doing out here in the first place.

But you do. Now head back, and you can continue your search when we get a new lead on her location, he replied.

You're fucking useless. I growled back.

Not as useless as you're going to be if you can't get your ass in gear and find the girl. He snickered.

You know what? I'll dump her off on the first guard I find. I shot back with venom.

Kelvin is a terrible choice. Vampire or not, he's got a nasty temper. He laughed as his voice vanished.

I growled at the thought. With a wave of my hand, I opened a portal under my feet and dropped back into the Dome.

The Dome was a safe haven for those who sought respite from the soulless. Some believed angels would descend from Heaven to help them fight the war. But when their call was left unanswered, we gods that were deemed fake or useless decided to step in and assist in any way we could.

The memory of my disciples calling upon us flashed through the back of my mind, but only a few stepped forward to help our awakened spirits. Ra, Osiris, Asherah, and myself had exchanged harsh words about the humans before we decided to answer the call for help after I'd been given the task to seek out the one who would restore the Earth. Anubis had lent his army to me, but he decided this was not his war to fight.

~~ Six Years Prior~~

"This is their own undoing. Do you not know how these humans operate down there?" Horus the elder shouted at me.

I rolled my eyes with my arms folded over my chest. "You realize that this could be the end of the human race as it is? Don't you get it? Without them we are nothing. Who are we to lead when there is no one to lead?"

A blue Avian named Atlas, a good ole friend of mine, had swooped down from the skies, landing beside me, his breath labored.

"You okay?" Asherah asked, taking a step toward him.

Atlas shook his head while he regained control of his breathing. "No, one of our fugitives is on the loose and he was last seen here." He huffed.

"What does he look like?" Ra asked.

"I have no idea, he's changed his look so many times but with all of this going on, he might expose himself." He swallowed hard.

Horus and Isis scoffed, "You can have fun with this mouse hunt of yours Asherah, I will not be included in your demise." Horus the elder shook his head. He and Isis took off to the sky, leaving Ra, Anubis, Asherah and several others behind.

Anubis turned his eyes to the sky then over to me. "Well Seth, it looks like you have your hands full. I will not personally get involved in this… but you can borrow as many undead as you need."

I glanced over at Anubis, giving him a curt nod, "I appreciate that. But for now, I need to find this mystery woman."

"I will stand with you." Ra commented.

"You don't have much of a choice, God of Creation." Asherah giggled. "I need to be around anyways for this girl, so I'll be here as well."

"Well, it looks like I'll be sticking around to watch you fail again, Seth." Osiris beamed me the most ridiculous smile.

I pinched the bridge of my nose and inhaled a sharp breath. "Anyone else?" I asked.

The other shook their heads, disappearing into the sky as Horus and Isis did before them.

"Well, I guess we should get this going then. No more time to waste."

"I'll work with Portú to get the Revival Ritual started then." Ra chimed in, stepping back into a beam of light.

~~End Flashback~~

Once I arrived, I tilted my head to the sky and took in a breath of fresh air. The skies were clear, and the sun shone down on those we'd managed to rescue before the Soulless got heir hands on them. Vampires and wolves to nymphs, fairies, and everything in between had taken refuge here. I headed off to the building to report my findings to a man Ra had put in charge of everyone. His demeanor was disgusting when it came to the feminine mythics and spirituals, but what the God of creation says… goes.

The buzzing of little wings beside my head caused me to shake my head. "Will you cut it out, Opal? You sound like a fly when you do that," I snapped, turning my head in the direction of the baby dragon. His wings were massive compared to his tiny serpent body. Opal's scales glistened with iridescent colors in the light. His bright orange eyes blinked in confusion as he focused on me.

"Why are you in a foul mood, Seth? Did you lose her again?" Opal snickered before flying off.

"Why is everyone acting like this is such an easy task?" I stomped off with Cyrus hot on my heels.

"Don't let Opal get to you. He's not even an adult yet. But even then, Seth, you're the God of chaos and trickery, remember?" Cyrus said as the pitter-patter of her large paws on the grass shifted to clicking with each step as we entered the plain marble building.

"You lost her again, Seth? Are you fucking trying to piss me off today?" a man's voice shouted as I rounded the corner.

My combat boots shrieked to a halt on the marble as I craned my head in the direction of the voice. "Excuse me? Who the fuck do you think you're talking to?" I turned and stalked toward the figure I thought went with the voice and came face to face with a man.

Something was fishy about him; his abilities were unknown. All I'd have to do was drag him to the deepest depths of the underworld and throw him into a labyrinth without a guide. His soul would surely rot.

An evil smirk formed on his lips. "Seth, the oh mighty lord of the desert or whatever you are. You know you can't do a thing to me. Surely Ra would punish you for your actions towards me."

"Ra will see through your treachery one day, Overlord." I grumbled.

"You know what? I'm sick of your voice. Let's just silence you for a bit, shall we?" With a wave of his hand, a tightening sensation formed around the front of my throat.

I tried to speak, but only a harsh breath left my lips. My eyes widened at the realization that my vocal cords were tied.

You son of a bitch.

The Overlord pointed and laughed. "Oh my, this is a sight to see!"

I took a step forward, only to be stopped by a bright light. As I brought my arm up to shield my eyes, Ra's voice emanated from the light.

"Seth, you know better than that," Ra nagged.

I let out a soundless growl before taking off towards my home. I decided to walk rather than use a portal. It had been a few years since I had taken in what the world had become inside this place. As I made my way through the fields, I tried to clear my throat and yell, shout, or even whisper anything. But it was no use. I slammed my fist into the closest tree, puncturing it straight through. A small, red-haired pixie dropped from it as it shook.

"Hey! I was trying to sleep!" the little one screamed.

I shook my head and waved her off as I watched the hole in the tree slowly stitch itself back together

This is fucking ridiculous I sent to Ra.

Now Seth, you need to keep focused. Don't worry about the Overlord. I'm sure he will untie your cords soon.

Ra. Of course, he always seemed to have something to say.

You already know he won't.

It's not like you're a man of many words anyway, Seth. Think of this as an exercise of sorts.

You're really trying my patience, Ra. Why the fuck did you even put him in charge instead of Osiris?

Ha, you think I could trust Osiris? He's been throwing a fit since this war broke out

That makes sense, but why this bastard?

He's a mythic and he seemed to have this leadership stuff down, so I figured why not. You had no interest in taking this responsibility. Quit your fussing.

Ra, I swear. If I had known, I would have gladly taken the damn responsibility. Trickster or not, that idiot is going to get us all killed.

Silence was my only reply as I stepped into my building. I sighed loudly and scanned the living room--a simple, tan-colored loveseat and recliner faced one another with a small coffee table between them. It was rare that I had any interactions with anyone within the Dome, and I preferred a single floor home rather than an overwhelmingly large space. I turned to the kitchen. Granted it was small because as a God in this world I rarely needed to eat.

I ran a hand through my hair after removing my helmet. *I need to prepare for her arrival. I'm coming for you, and this time, I won't be coming back without you.*

Stalking off to the bathroom, I quickly pulled my gear off and stripped down before walking around the frosted glass wall in front of the shower. I cranked the knob to turn it on, not caring what temperature it landed on.

I leaned against the side wall and stared off into space, the stream of water softly drumming against my skin. *What am I going to do? How long is it going to take for me to get everything ready for the revival? We are running out of time.* I tried to in anger, only for a harsh nothingness to escape my lips. What the fuck was I supposed to do?

--

Six more years passed, and I watched as the world descend further into chaos. The city of Milpitas, located in a state called California, there were still humans running around seeking shelter in their gas masks as they drove around in their armored vehicles scavenging for supplies and food.

What are they doing? Are they unchanged? I wondered, poking my head from around the corner of what seemed to be a liquor store.

Cyrus sat by my feet awaiting my command

I started to take a step out of the cover of darkness in the alleyway when the dull moans and groans of the Soulless om ahead. I immediately froze and stepped back into the shadows and watched a horde of the Soulless charged the vehicle parked out front.

I scanned the small horde and noticed a man running toward the front door. He was missing bits of his left hand from the wrist down and was riddled in deep wounds like those from a knife. My eyes then landed on a woman, whose eyes reflected no indication of cognitive function. Bits of her flesh were peeling from her face and leg. The Soulless woman released a shrieking cry as she clawed at the passenger door of the vehicle.

Cyrus's voice popped into my head. *Well, what do you want to do? These humans are exposed to those things, and we can't afford to lose anymore.*

These people are going to get themselves killed.

That's basically what I just said.

Will you shut up?

Will you use your brain for once?

I'm beginning to regret keeping you around.

No you're not. Go save their asses and I'll wait for you here.

I shook my head, sick of the whole situation. Unholstering my .45, I took aim as I stepped out of the shadows once more.

I squeezed the trigger again and again, and the two humans in the vehicle gawked at the sight as I mowed down the small group. I pushed my visor up and jutted my head in the direction of the store.

Hurry and grab what you need. I'll keep watch out here, I said to them through telepathy.

The two didn't hesitate as they scrambled out of the vehicle with their gas masks and grabbed what they needed.

Some time passed, and the streets grew quiet as a few of the operable streetlights flickered, giving the empty street an eerie feeling. I wondered what had happened to the humans and turned to walk into the store to find them picking and choosing over the leftover snacks.

Will you two hurry the hell up? Those things are going to come back soon and you two need to go! I sent them a warning since my vocal cords were still tied.

The two scrambled to grab their supplies, headed straight to their vehicle, and sped out of the parking lot. I turned and began to walk out and stopped as my gaze landed on a red canned beverage labeled "Monster" I shook my head at the label and grabbed it.

They don't know what a monster is. I chuckled to myself as I cracked the can open and gulped down the fruity taste. Crushing the can, I simply tossed it to the side and continued on. *Now, where were we?*

Lead after lead had turned up nothing, and I was becoming more and more agitated, beginning to lose hope as I trudged through a forgotten city. It seemed I was somewhere North of my last location.

I cautiously moved through the city. My gaze fell upon dead bodies in the streets, burning vehicles, and buildings destroyed beyond repair.

The shriek of a man broke the silence in the air, causing me to pause for a moment as I honed in on the sound. I closed my eyes and let my senses lead me to an abandoned skyscraper. I stopped at the entrance and inhaled a sharp breath. Unprecedented fear poured into my veins.

A dull ache coursed through my chest and struck my heart. Ignoring the pain, I glanced up at the building before me and scanned it from the floor, ground up to the top.

Where am I? What is going on? a feminine voice panicked in my head.

It's her! I thought as I entered the building. With my .45 mm handgun drawn and loaded, I traveled through the maze of hallways. *I'm coming for you. I just hope I'm not too late this time*, I thought to myself as the grumbles and dull moans of the soulless rushed ahead of me. I followed their lead, stepping over the bodies of those recently departed only to stop at the end of one hallway.

There she was behind the glass, her beautiful sapphire blue eyes wide with fear and softened with the acceptance of death. My heart throbbed as I kept my gaze on her. The woman's snow-white hair framed her round face and fell at her sides. Her tanned, petite hands clutched her light pink gown, which stopped just below her knees. She was the most beautiful woman I had ever seen.

I'm here. No need to fret, little one. I smiled to myself under the visor of my helmet.

Chapter 4: Consciousness

Iris

Muffled banging thumped before me. I sat petrified. Hordes of zombie-like creatures were attempting to break the glass that held me captive. My body shook as waves of overwhelming fear poured through my veins like water from an open hydrant.

"What the hell are those things?" My voice trembled. My lower lip quivered. Every fiber of my being screamed for me to run, but where? Never in my life had I given my death a second thought.

I quickly backed away from the glass and gasped when my back pressed against the opposing wall. My knees buckled, causing me to fall to the cold hard floor. My heart pounded in my ears.

These... these had to be the casualties, like I was about to be. I thought back to what the soldier had told me about the war before he burst into flames. The chemical reaction from whatever those beings sprayed had begun changing humans into these Soulless creatures. Those who were blessed by some spiritual magic or were deities hiding amongst them were the only ones that remained unchanged, such as myself. According to the conversation I happened to overhear.

I had only caught a glimpse of this war during my transport. I'd been and out of consciousness during the flights and evacuations.

A spider-web crack marred the surface of the glass holding me captive gave way as it gave way with the force from dozens of pounding hands, and the Soulless creatures in front of me increased the fury of their blows. My breath quickened, and tears poured from my eyes. Finally, the compromised glass slowly buckled under their assault.

I yelped in fear, covering my face when the barrier shattered. Glass hit the floor. The images before me played in slow motion, and time seemed to trickle to a stop. A gunshot roared from behind the horde. A bullet pierced the man in front of me the moment he lunged.

His blood splattered against my skin and my eyes widened. I touched my face with a trembling hand, wiping the blood away my eyes located then fixated on a single man wearing what looked like riot gear from head to toe. In his hand, a single handgun was pointed at the swarm before me. He fired round after round, and my attackers fell like flies until none remained.

I released my breath. With blurry eyes, I gazed at the corpse in front of me, letting out a silent cry. I panted and panic finally released its hold on me. A series of sobs and whimpers left my lips, my body frozen in fear as the slow and steady clicking of the man's boots approached me. He crouched in front of me, and my muscles tensed.

A hand appeared below my chin. I gasped at the touch as he forced my head to tilt up. I couldn't build enough courage to look at him and kept my gaze to the floor. He gave my head a sudden jerk as if to say, 'Look at me.' I could hear his steady breath against the visor of his helmet. Another sudden jerk caused my eyes to shoot up from the floor and land where I guessed his eyes were. The tint on the visor blocked my ability to see through it.

My lips parted and I sucked in a breath at my reflection: a flash of blue cut across his visor. I did not have time to process what I saw as I pulled away from him and quickly pushed myself off the floor. Sparks fired off in my head. Something inside of me had awakened. I groaned, gripping the sides of my head. There was pressure, a hand on my lower back, and I turned toward the man. He placed his hand over my mouth, effectively silencing me. I grabbed his wrist and squeezed.

The man's head jolted up as he maneuvered me behind him. He quickly ejected the empty magazine from his gun and reloaded it before taking aim. I gripped the back of his belt loops and shut my eyes tightly, flinching with every shot that rang in my ears.

Each shot caused the throbbing to worsen, and they pounded until my muscles went limp. A hand caught my head before it could hit the cold floor.

I remained conscious, thoughts racing as my eyes locked onto the man. His focus would switch between me and whatever became a target in his eyes. My vision blurred, by the time the firing ceased, my breath ragged.

The black-clad man knelt beside me and placed his fingers on my neck. With a nod, he seemed satisfied that my pulsing artery had given him the response he was looking for. He checked his watch, then raised the visor on his helmet.

Our eyes met. Swirling green orbs stared back at me—an expression of worry displayed across them.

A wave of pain coursed through me, causing me to arch my back. I shut my eyes and withheld my scream. My mind replayed scenes of water and waves from the ocean, then shifted to the harsh winds of the desert. I reached for the man and grabbed his hand. My core burned. I needed something, but what?

The man pulled his visor back down and lifted me bridal style. I clutched onto his hand as he carried me out of my makeshift prison.

A gust of wind brushed against me, but only for a moment, then the man growled with anger.

Resting my head against his chest, I could hear his faint but steady heartbeat through his Kevlar and clothing. I felt an overwhelming sense of safety and melted into him, steadying my breath as the flame inside of me grew.

"Is this her?" A harsh voice invaded my ears. "It'd better be. You know how long it took to figure out where she was held captive this time?" it shouted.

The man holding me didn't answer and simply nodded as he began walking again. The crunching of rocks under his boots turned into shuffling across what sounded like grass. I let out a small sigh of relief when the overwhelming sense of death that loomed over me dissipated.

Another wave of pain coursed through my body as my muscles tensed Scenes of the ocean, the high winds blowing through a forest, even a grassy plain flashed in the back of my mind. I let out a small cry and brought my hand to my stomach. The ground rose to meet my back, and a cool sensation then pressed against my forehead. I opened my eyes. To my surprise, my savior's bare hand was pressed against my forehead.

His hands are cold, but his body is warm... How is that possible? I took a closer look.

My eyes widened at the realization that the man before me was not human. His cool, gray skin screamed Underworld, but his energy told a different story.

"Who are you?" I asked with a shaky breath. Ignoring the pain as best as I could, I propped myself onto my elbows and tried to roll onto my side to sit up. He shifted his hand behind my back as support. The man shook his head and reached up with his free hand to remove his helmet. He pulled it off and ran a hand through his hair. He opened his eyes, and I could not believe the emerald orbs that stared back at me once more. It was neither a dream nor an illusion, but this man resembled a god.

I was at a loss for words. His jawline was slender, holding a neatly trimmed beard which told me he was very well kept. His hair was a dark brown, cut short, but due to the excessive sweat from the helmet he wore, it was damp and stuck to his skin.

A sharp pain stabbed at the base of my neck, and coursed down to the center of my chest, and traveled even farther down to my navel, causing me to lurch forward, holding my chest as I yelped. The man pulled my hand from my stomach and replaced it with his own. The pain settled to a mere ache. My gaze volleyed from his eyes to his hand.

How did he do that? I wondered. My lips parted to speak, but nothing came out. The man then leaned towards my side. His lips were inches away from my ear as his breath fanned my skin, but he did not speak. His silence sent a wave of calming emotions through to my core, settling the fire that was kindling within me.

I took in a deep breath and exhaled before he pulled himself away from my ear. The man then gazed over his shoulder; his eyes fixated on a light in the distance. He let out a short but heavy sigh and shook his head before rising with his hand extended.

I looked at his hand then at his eyes. It was as if he was speaking to me through his energy. Something told me to take his hand. Reaching up and placing my hand in his, he pulled me gently to my feet and scooped me up again. With his foot, he maneuvered his helmet as if he were kicking up a hacky sack. As it fell, it landed right onto his head perfectly. Impressed, I blinked a few times to reassure myself that I was not dreaming.

The man pressed my head against his chest and motioned for me to hold on. I reached up to his Kevlar and held on as tight as I could. A black hole opened in the ground. My heart leaped into my throat as we made the drop, only to resurface inside a building.

I peeped through one eye when we stopped moving, my heart pounded in my ears. My gaze scanned the area, the inside of this building was laced in white marble and black granite with bare walls and minimal furniture. When I finally deemed the place safe, I looked up at the man. His head was turned to the side, staring at something... or rather, someone.

THE WAR BETWEEN

The clicking of heeled shoes approached from my blind spot. The man holding me turned and set me down on my feet before clenching his fists. I clutched my gown, and a sense of anxiety and overwhelming fear washed over me in waves. My breath was lost to the silence.

I searched for the footsteps' source and eventually landed on another man standing adjacent to the one who had brought me here. His black hair was slicked back, his yellow eyes bored holes into my soul as he stared, and his pale skin remained exposed through his unbuttoned shirt. The man flashed a toothy grin.

Whispers broke out through the room amongst those who lingered. I stopped staring at the man and focused my erratic senses on the whispers.

"It's her."

"He found her."

"We can win the war."

"Is it really her?"

Beads of sweat formed along my neck and forehead as the fire in my core ignited once more.

The strange man knelt in front of me and smiled. "So, he was successful in finding you! I've been searching for you for some time now, just like the others. You can call me the Overlord, if you like." Rubbing his chin with a smirk across his face. "Where have you been hiding?"

Why does this man look familiar? I thought. From his height to his build, the man looked like someone I had seen before. Something in the back of my mind clicked. *No it can't be. Is this the man who held me captive all of this time?*

I gulped as I pulled my voice from the pocket it seemed to have jumped into. "I d-don't know. I don't remember much besides being moved constantly. I just woke up in a room with glass walls. The next thing I know, I saw a horde of those... things. What are they?"

The man stroked his beard and clicked his tongue. "So, you don't remember the war, do you?" he asked. The vibration of his voice caused my skin to prickle with goosebumps.

I took a deep breath, and the pain in my core poured into my veins. With each beat of my heart, my body throbbed in agony. I couldn't understand why I was in so much pain. The man's eyes never left mine as his gaze scanned over my figure.

The fire grew, and my face slowly contorted in pain. Why was I reacting like this?

The man chuckled and rose. "This woman is to remain in my care. Do you understand? In this timeline, she is mine," he said to the man beside me. A smirk crossed his lips.

I angled my head up to look at the man who saved me, and even with his visor down, I could feel his sense of anger toward the Overlord. As if he knew what this man was intending to do.

What does that mean? What is he going to do to me? Panic rose in my heart as I searched my body for any indication of pregnancy. My eyes widened as I failed to find any stretch marks or the darkened line that should have run down my stomach. "I really am in a different timeline," I whispered to myself.

"Is there something you're looking for?" the Overlord asked with piqued interest.

"What year are we in? You mentioned a war. Is that what happened? Where are my kids? My husband? My family? Where are they?"

The man clenched his jaw. In a flash, he reached for me and grabbed my arm, pulling me tight against him. "I can't tell you that. In this timeline, you're pure, innocent, and have no children or a husband," he growled at me as he pulled me away from my savior.

I struggled to free from his grasp, only for his grip around my wrist to tighten. *Help me, please! You can't let him take me!* I pleaded with my expression towards the man I felt safe with. His gaze toward me was apologetic. He could not go against this man who was pulling me away from him.

A forceful tug of my arm sent me flying into a room. The left side of my body slammed against the floor, causing my muscles and joints to scream in agony. Something in my arm gave way with a searing pop.

"What was that for?" I coughed and cried out, clutching my injured arm. I lay my head on the cold floor and winced with every move I made. I rolled onto my back with my eyes shut and held my dislocated limb.

Through the darkness, I could see my savior, his emerald eyes staring back at me with fear. Did this man feel for me? In this short amount of time, did something spark in him, too? Tears welled in my eyes as a firm hand gripped my face. My eyes shot open, and a pair of bright yellow orbs greeted me.

"Get away from me." My voice cracked, and I struggled to push him away with my uninjured arm.

He smirked. "Or what?" He slipped his hand over my mouth. "You'll think twice about disobeying me." He leaned down and pressed his lips to my neck just behind my ear, which triggered a tensed response from my body. The images that once flashed in my mind slowly faded.

With his free hand, he worked his way down from my waist under my blood-stained dress, his cold hand hovered over my lower abdomen. I froze when his hands touched my solar plexus. My breath hitched, and I began to shake.

"It's going to be difficult for you to do anything with this pain isn't it? And your power will be locked away until I say so." He chuckled as he pressed his hand firmly against my skin.

The pain intensified, causing me to arch my back in an intense spasm. *Help me, please!* I screamed in my head.

You can do that yourself, a voice responded.

I can't! I cried back.

But you can, it replied.

I squeezed my eyes shut and mustered up the courage to fight back. With a deep breath through my nose, I exhaled the loudest scream I could produce. The sound waves that escaped from my lips caused the Earth to shake. The floor beneath me opened, and I fell through. I screamed in fear as I kept falling.

A light shined below me, and a sense of safety enveloped me. A pair of strong arms wrapped around me in the darkness, cradling me. I gazed up to see Seth without his helmet. Those beautiful emerald-green eyes shone bright in the darkness.

I've got you.

Chapter 5: Reported Findings

Overlord

I stood with my hand in my pocket and with the other I stroked my chin. I chuckled at the sight as I stared into the chasm that woman had created. "My, my, this one is certainly the one we've been looking for isn't it." I smiled to myself.

Pulling my phone out of my pocket, I dialed my original's number and waited for him to answer.

His voice immediately poured through the other end. "I hope you have news for me, Overlord."

I laughed for a moment. "Indeed I do. The mutt finally found her and brought her back. I wonder which facility she was in because he was able to find her with ease."

"Oh? She must have killed her guards then and that poor bastard of a chemist I sent to keep an eye on her," he replied nonchalantly.

"It doesn't matter. I've locked away her other two abilities for now. I don't know how long it'll hold for but if you're coming to get her, you need to do it quickly," I shot back with venom.

"You should know better than to talk back to me. Remember who you are. I could have you killed just like that," he snapped.

I let out a low growl and huffed as I rolled my eyes. I knew I was this man's clone, he told me when I emerged from my artificial womb.

The problem is, I didn't feel human at all. How did this fool think he was human when I carried his DNA. He's done nothing special to me when he created me.

"Scary threat there, Ian. Better be ready when they land in New York in a few months. I can't guarantee I'll be sticking around to do any more of your bidding." I removed the phone from my ear and disconnected the call.

Chapter 6: Buried Feelings

Seth

The Overlord and I exchanged glances before I teleported to catch the woman after her scream shook the Earth and created a chasm right below her.

"Lock her away upstairs until I figure out what to do with her, Seth." He smirked as I teleported into a room on one of the secure levels of the main building. I laid her down on the bed and stepped out, shutting the door behind me.

Are you really going to listen to that man? Even if Ra put him in charge of this safe haven, you had a duty to this woman. Not him.

Ra put the man in charge; he can figure out what to do with her.

She needs you, Seth. Not him. Asherah's voice rang in the back of my mind.

What do you mean, Asherah? What did he do to her?

You know what I mean. Don't act so innocent. She chuckled. *It seems he's tied her abilities, like he did your voice. I fear her life is in danger if you even think to leave her with him.*

You mean I need to…

You're going to have to break that seal that the Overlord bound her with. But I am certain that in this case, love will do the trick. Trust me, you'll figure it out.

I really hate this game.

You'll be just fine.

Watching from outside the glass room the Overlord had instructed me to keep her in, I began to panic. I didn't know if this was even the right girl, but my soul sang to me, confirming everyone's thoughts. I couldn't bear the thought of any harm coming to her. I found myself pacing as anxiety flooded my veins.

How could this man tell me she is to remain under his protection, yet the rules don't apply to him? How can he harm her and cause so much pain and not face any consequences? Why her? Who is she?

Asherah had approached me when the darkness clouded the skies and told me who I needed to find, but she'd never given me a name or an idea of what she would look like. She told me I would know once I found her, to follow my instinct, and that it would lead me to who I sought out. Lo and behold, here she was, writhing in pain.

I couldn't help her, and I felt utterly useless. The God of chaos and trickery, and I couldn't even bring a woman out of her misery. I stopped pacing the hall and turned to face her as her expression contorted in pain and agony. Something pushed me to help. *But how?* The only thing that could soothe her was touch. Granted, putting her shoulder back into place would cause her even more pain.

I clenched my fist and slammed it into the control panel on the door. *Fuck it,* I thought to myself and stripped off my helmet and shirt as I opened the door. The woman was curled into the fetal position, and her screams pulled at my heart. I studied her figure and tried to hold back every temptation to turn around and kill that man. But I knew deep down inside she needed me to protect her, as Asherah had said. But first and foremost, her current dilemma; her shoulder needed to be put back in place.

I stalked up to the side of the bed and placed my hand on hers. The woman's muscles tensed against my touch. Her cries died down to mere whimpers as I rolled her onto her back. She was still holding onto her arm. I leaned forward to the crook of her neck and breathed slowly, cooling her neck.

Calm down. I know you're in pain. I'm here to help. I soothed her through the energy I emitted, since I still could not speak.

She relaxed to the best of her ability as my hands glided over her shoulder and the center of her chest. The pain radiating from her slowly disappeared. She let out a ragged breath.

Let me help you with this. It isn't my intention to bring you any harm. But I need to put your joint back in place. I pushed my thoughts toward her.

The woman's eyes shot open. Her petrified expression told me she didn't want to. But we both knew it had to be done, or another wave of pain would most certainly push her over the edge.

"I can't," she whispered. "Everything hurts. Why? Why did he do this to me? What did he mean when he said the pain would be too much?" She wept. Her tears flowed down her cheeks and onto the bedspread.

Please don't cry. I soothed once again as I eased her into a sitting position.

Her hand grabbed mine, squeezing gently. She whimpered and nodded frantically.

Please... hurry.

Easy. Remember; calm. Stay calm and relax.

She took a deep breath and exhaled it slowly as I pulled the shoulder of her gown down exposing the obvious dislocation.

What's going on? I'm so dizzy.

It seems that you have a pinched nerve that could be causing it. I can make that, and the pain go away. Is that what you wish?

What? How?

Just give me a moment and you'll see.

I sat on the edge of the bed and gently turned her left side to face me. *Take a deep breath. This is going to hurt for a moment.*

I gripped her tiny arm just above her elbow with my other arm wrapped around her. *You ready?* I asked, gazing down at her.

She took in a deep breath and loosened as much tension as best as she could. *I... I'm ready.*

Here we go. I squeezed her like an accordion while pushing her joint back into its socket with a loud pop. I didn't wait for her reaction as I pulled her to my chest and lulled away her pain. She gripped my arm and let out a silent cry. Her body shook.
I gave her a minute, sitting in silence waiting for her body to calm back down. After a short period of time, she exhaled and sank further into my arms.
Glancing down at her I raised a brow at her. *How's the pain?*
Gone... How did you?

Your body speaks, even when you don't.

How is it that I can understand you?

Because your brain and mine are connected. I speak through telepathy, as do you. Even if I could talk, you would be afraid of me, always. You see, my voice is... almost demon-like. And the things I've done are unspeakable.

THE WAR BETWEEN

Why can't you speak? And why would I fear you? Who are you, really?

The one put in charge of the safety of people like you sealed my vocal cords. I cannot speak. And you would fear me because I am the God of the trickery, chaos, the protector of the dead.

Her body tensed against mine.

Wait. Are you really the God of Chaos?

I sighed and placed her on the bed before rising. I kept my back to her as I revealed my proper form. Blackish blue fur sprouted from my face, neck, and ears, as my human ears formed a set of triangular ones atop my head. The snout of a dog shifted from my nose and mouth, which sprouted sharp canines.

Promise you won't scream?

I can't make that promise.

I peeked over my shoulder at her to gauge her expression before I revealed my entire face. For some reason, I felt nervous. I actually cared about what she thought of me. From her raised eyebrows, I could tell she wasn't afraid. If anything, her interest was piqued.

Taking a deep breath, I turned around and revealed myself to her. She gasped, bringing her hand to her mouth as her blue eyes scanned me from head to toe.

You're beautiful! Wait, you have the head of a... Wait.

Yes, I'm Seth.

My guardian literally is the God of... How in the living hell did this—

The clicking of heels paraded down the hall, causing me to shift back quickly. I ran for the door and opened it, scooping up my things from the floor. I left in such a hurry I didn't close the door behind me.

After making it back to my room, I changed my sweat-soaked clothing and headed back to her room. *Shit, I forgot to ask— Wait... where did she... ?* I groaned and threw my helmet on before stomping off to find her. It was relatively easy to follow her scent, which lingered all over my skin.

After taking a few turns through the clusters of hallways and down a set of stairs to the first floor, I finally caught up to the woman as she prepared to run through the last set of doors to the outside.

Where are you going? I asked, reaching out to her

I'm leaving. I can't stay here.

What happened when I left.

That man says I have to go back over to the central area of the building... A room closer to his. Tears threatened to spill from her eyes as she turned away and took off.

Wait! I reached out to her, but she didn't stop. I took off towards the main building, my fists clenched. Harming a woman was never the correct answer in any situation. But the Overlord going back on his own instructions? It was an even bigger offense in my book, and I wasn't about to let this piece of shit scare off our only means of survival.

Don't do it, Seth, Ra's voice sounded in the back of my mind.

Why does he even want her? If this fucking task was given to me, then why the fuck does he demand for me to bring her to him? Why?

Ra paused for a moment; confusion pushed through to my mind from his as we both sat wondering what was actually going on.

Seth, what do you mean?

You know exactly what I mean. He's been bitching about me bringing her to him for the last twelve years. Why? What is so special about this woman that he wants her for himself? I was given this task, not him.

That... I have no words for.

Now, you saw what he did. He's going to die, I growled back.

Yes, I saw what he did. But if you kill him, it could change the timeline, he replied with haste.

Fuck the timeline, Ra. You saw what he fucking did! I will not stand by and watch him kill her, I roared.

He sighed heavily. *Fine. I'll be down shortly.*

I rounded the final corner to the main building. Rage pumped through my veins with every beat of my heart. In the center of the room stood the Overlord, his eyes fixated on me.

"You dare challenge my word?" he shouted, his voice echoing through the empty room.

I removed my helmet and threw it at him. It hit him square in the chest before he could react, knocking him to the ground and leaving him gasping for air.

You will die if you ever lay a hand on her again, I sent to the Overlord, stomping over to where he was sprawled on the ground.

A light brighter than the sun appeared between the Overlord and me.

"Boys, let's not get too upset now," Ra's voice sounded from the fading light.

Ra's tall and thin figure appeared wearing a sun-shaped headdress and a white robe laced in gold silk.

A growl vibrated my chest as the Overlord slowly managed to rise from the floor, clutching his heart.

"Is the mutt mad that I got to his girl before he did? Or did you not get a taste of her yet?" he mocked.

I got a lot farther than you did, and still managed to take away her pain. So keep talking. The only reason you're still alive is because of Ra. You come near her or even breathe in her direction again and I'll kill you, I replied, smirking.

Ra pinched the bridge of his wrinkled nose and turned to the Overlord. "You know better than to touch, let alone assault, a woman ever. Seth is in charge of her care and protection, not you. You're lucky he didn't kill you the moment you laid a hand on her. The only reason he didn't is because any drastic changes in this timeline could change everything!" he roared. "You are relieved of your duties. Better yet... " Ra turned his attention to me and nodded

The timeline won't be affected if he happens to just... Disappear. I grinned.

Go get the girl-- but be careful of her emotions right now; she's very delicate-- and we will handle this when you get back. Oh, and by the way. Her name is Iris.

Iris, huh. I wasn't expecting a name like that.
Shut up and go.

I shifted my gaze to the Overlord, then back to Ra before opening a portal to Iris's location. I scanned the area before my eyes landed on a building just outside of the Dome. An overwhelming sense of dread and fear radiated from the building.

Shaking my head, I checked my firearm to make sure it was locked and loaded as I headed into the building. Iris's scent gave me a trail through the trashed and discarded hallways. A wave of worry washed over me as I became more concerned about this woman's safety. Why couldn't I shake the feeling that Iris was something more than just someone I was ordered to protect? Would I have felt the same way if I had found her on my own without the threat of this war?

Where are you?

How did you find me? she replied with a huff.

Your scent is all over me, remember?

Oh my God, this is embarrassing.

Hey, all I did was give you a bear hug of sorts. Now, where the hell are   *you?*

You will have to drag me out of here!

Would you please stop being so difficult? And if I have to drag you out of here, then so be it. But we have to go.

I'm not going back there! She cried.

A growl vibrated my chest as I stalked through the hallways. The soulless' growing chatter became louder and louder with each corner I turned, signaling that I was closing the distance between Iris and me.

I pressed my back against the wall right before a corner and peeked around it to count the soulless with my firearm in hand.

Twenty-two isn't terrible. Double-checking my extended magazine, I turned the corner and began firing off rounds. Headshot after headshot, their bodies dropped to the floor. I brought my gaze from the floor to the end of the hallway and saw a glass room like the one back at the main building.

I skipped over the dead bodies and into the room. To my surprise, the door was wide open. Straightening my posture, I approached the bed with caution, only to find a large leather trunk between the bed and an old desk. I focused my line of sight through the material and looked straight at her.

You coming? I asked, raising a brow at her.

Iris shook her head at me, tears pouring down her face.

Annoyed, I leaned down and flipped the lid open and gently pulled her out, placing her on the bed.

We can't keep meeting like this, I joked and tried to lighten the situation.

I can't go back there! Iris sobbed.

Well, I have no choice. We have to go back, I stated.

Why can't you just let me die?

Because if you die, we all do. How about this? You come back with me, and I kill that bastard.

Y-you'd do that for me?

I don't see why not?

Iris placed her head in her hands and sobbed even louder. I reached down and rubbed her back in understanding.

Then a sickening crack echoed from the end of the hallway. The woman jumped to her feet. A fit of anger rose in me, but then I realized this anger was hers.

Why me? She glanced up at me, stomping her feet in a child-like fit. I could see the muscles in her neck tense, a little blue light glowed as she brought her hands to the sides of her head.

A mutated soulless creature with open sores covered in spilled blood shuffled its way down the corridor, its bones cracking with each step. I reached for the woman's arm, and she pulled away from me. As her arm swung, tears from her cheeks began to float and shoot out of the room as if they were bullets aimed at the creature.

Blood poured from its wounds, its knees buckled, and it sank to the floor. My eyes widened when I turned to face her.

She turned to me, her jaw dropping *What the fuck was that?*

I was just about to ask you the same thing... I shrugged.

Didn't that man say he was going to lock my abilities away? Yet I fucking wield water? That's what's so special about me?

All I could do was shrug my shoulders. *I guess so…*

She grabbed my arm and shook me. "What do you mean, you guess so? Ugh!"

I winced, plugging my ear with my finger at the loudness of her voice. *Why are you shouting?"*

Iris narrowed her eyes at me. I could feel the anger radiating from her. "Because I am livid!" she screamed, her made the Earth's surface quiver.

I remained as patient as I could and exhaled a long breath. I jabbed my thumb towards the exit, giving her an indication that it was time to go. She took one look at me and shook her head.

"I'm not going anywhere-- not until you tell me what the hell is so special about me." She crossed her arms and planted her feet.

You're acting like a child. If I had all of the answers, don't you think I would have told you by now? Because you are refusing to come back with me, the one person who has those answers for you is becoming impatient.

"Wait… Who?"

You'll have to see, but it's not the Overlord, if that's what you're thinking. I scooped her into my arms and dropped into a portal back to the border of the Dome in an attempt to calm her before meeting with Ra. I set Iris down, a huff escaping her lips. I glanced down at her hands and discovered they were clenched into tight fists.

What's wrong? I asked. That familiar worry springing up again

Nothing you'd care about.

Unfortunately, I have to care about what's upsetting you.

Well, this isn't something you can... fix.

Try me.

Iris' head jolted up, and her sapphire blue eyes reflected sadness and confusion. Her emotions pulled at my heart and my mind as her bottom lip trembled. A small white light glowed on her forehead, causing me to step back.

What the--?

I have no idea how I ended up here... I--I lost everything. My kids, husband, family, and hell, I don't even know my own name.

The crunching of leaves and snapping twigs pulled us from our thoughts. We both turned to face an oncoming horde of the soulless. I quickly reloaded, but as I took aim, Iris twirled her finger. The air around us formed a tornado, picking up debris, uprooting trees, and the Soulless. With one wave of her hand, she sent the entire tornado towards one of the forgotten cities.

"Wind," she simply said. "Water and wind. Don't tell me, I can use fire, too?" She glared at me as she spun on one heel and stalked off toward the Dome. I couldn't believe what I'd witnessed, and my heart began to flutter. *Oh my, this is going to be an exciting turn of events for us!*
I quickly followed after her and grabbed her hand before opening a portal to my tiny home on the other side of the Dome. The warmth of her skin against mine caused my heart to jump into my throat.
The woman glanced down at our joined hands, and a small smile formed on her lips. "So, is this where you live when you're not out searching for me?" she asked.
I simply nodded and continued towards the door. I opened it and placed my hand on the small of the woman's back to usher her forward.
I have a spare room you can use so you're not anywhere near that bastard. And the goddess named Asherah made a wardrobe, which is in

there for you. I point over to the bathroom. *Go get cleaned up and I'll have everything ready for you before we go meet... Ra.*

"Did you just say Ra...? As in Egyptian God of creation and the sun?" She turned to me, wide eyed.

I nodded and ushered her towards the bathroom before closing the door behind her.

"You can't just tell me incredibly insane things and then not give me more than a nod!" she fussed as the sound of the shower turned on.

Yes, I can. I'm a God; there's plenty I can do. I smirked and strode into the guest room, stopping in front of the closet. I took a deep breath and swung the door open, to reveal rows of dresses and shoes for this woman.

What the hell am I doing? I thought to myself. I rolled my eyes, placing a hand on my hip and the other one through my hair. *Women and their clothing*, I thought once more as she finished rinsing off and came up behind me.

"Yeah, yeah, I get it, okay? We are very..." She trailed off as her eyes landed on the selection of dresses and shoes before her. "...picky."

I looked down at her. *You see what I mean?* I nudged Iris forward, only for my eyes to travel from her exposed nape down to her legs. I mouthed "wow" and turned around. The wet towel dropped to the floor with a light thud, and my curiosity got the best of me as I peeked over my shoulder at her slender, yet curvy figure.

Our eyes locked, and a light blush shaded her cheeks. I couldn't help but stare. My heart fluttered, and my mind went blank for a moment.
"Seth... you're staring," Iris whispered as she pulled a lilac-colored dress from the closet.
My apologies. In all of my life on this Earth, I've never... I stumble over my words and turned to walk out of the room. Images flashed

through my mind of the woman and me standing atop a mountain, a breeze blowing by as the world before us washed away in waves.

"Never what?" she asked. Her voice faded the further I walked out of the room.

My heart raced as I lost my breath. My lungs burned with each breath I took. Why was I feeling this invisible pull towards this woman again? How had I even found her in the first place? What was this feeling coursing through my veins? How did this woman feel safe with me, even though I guided souls to their final destination in death and had wreaked havoc upon Earth long ago? *Indeed, this is a mistake.*

I clenched my fist and slammed it into the wall, puncturing it easily.

Are you okay? What was that noise?

Nothing you'd be able to help with, I snarled.

Are you sure?

I eyed the hole in the wall. *Yes.*

A pair of slender arms wrapped around my hips, causing me to freeze as a sense of mortality washed over me. My heart slowed its pace, and my anger and confusion faded to a sense of calm.

I took in a deep breath before I turned around. The woman stepped back, and I couldn't help but smile. The long-sleeved lilac-colored gown she'd chosen hugged her curves in all the right places while hiding every secret she carried, yet a sense of power radiated from her.

We stood staring at one another for a moment before she cleared her throat, pulling me out of the trance her beauty had put me in.

Let's go, before I lose my mind. I ran my hand over my face. I couldn't believe this woman. *I don't know how I'm going to keep my hands off of this one.* I hoped she hadn't heard me, but telling from her shocked expression she had.

Her eyes widened, and her lips parted. *What? What did you say?*

I slapped my palm to my forehead. *Nothing... Seriously, let's go.*

Where? She tilted her head.

To kill the Overlord.

Chapter 7: Revealed

Iris

My eyes widened at his words. To kill the Overlord? Granted, I didn't like the guy— not in the slightest— but to kill the man? Could I bring myself to do it, or was this purely Seth?

"Speaking of which..." I pointed to his throat. "May I?"

May you what?

"I think I can help… Something inside of me is telling me to do this, so I'm going to do it." I stood on my tippy toes and gently pressed my index finger to his Adam's apple, causing him to flinch. "Please, trust me. I trusted you to help me, remember?" I closed my eyes and concentrated with my newfound water ability to locate the source of the tie.

I purred in thought, *He's just… so… hot.*

I heard that.

No, you didn't. The heat in my cheeks rose as butterflies fluttered in my stomach.

I slowly traced my finger down his throat until it was positioned just above his vocal cords and traced the shape of an R. "Release," I whispered. A one-inch area of his neck around my finger glowed blue, and the tie was released. I pulled my hand back and looked up at him.

Seth grabbed my hand midair as he cleared his throat, his gaze never shifting. "Thank you." His voice sounded a bit harsh, yet ethereal.

I blinked in confusion and nodded. "Of course. You've already saved me more times than I'd like to admit, so I wanted to return something to you. Now, let's go." I gave him a nervous chuckle as he scooped me into his arms.

I giggled when his hands grazed my skin.

"Why do you giggle? Did I say something funny?" His deep voice vibrated against my skin, causing me to giggle once more.

"Oh, no. It's just that I'm ticklish." I tucked my head into his chest and gripped his blue button-down shirt.

Seth scoffed at me before we dropped into a portal and reappeared in the marble-coated hell-hole. The room was silent, and I slowly opened my eyes in curiosity.

"That was fast," I whispered.

Yeah. Were you expecting a delay in time or something?

"Sort of? I have no idea what to expect from you," I replied.

Good, then I'll never cease to surprise you.

At this point, the conversation between us must have seemed odd to those eavesdropping. I decided to be vocal in my responses instead of speaking to Seth through our minds.

"Well, well. How nice of you to bring her back." The Overlord's voice sounded from behind Seth.

I froze and tightened my grip on Seth, who had yet to put me down.

Despite the sudden tension in his jaw, Seth gently put me down and spun around to face the Overlord, who was accompanied by another man in a white robe laced with gold and wearing a sun-shaped headdress.

My jaw hit the floor when I saw the other God present. "Ra..." I whispered as I cautiously stepped towards him. "It's really you. I thought Seth wasn't serious when he said we were coming to meet you."

Ra gave me a massive grin and he opened his arms. "Yes, Seth would never lie." He urged me to come forward.

"Careful, she's been tainted!" the Overlord snickered as I walked over to Ra.

"You may have touched her, but I get the honor of being in her presence," Seth shot back. "Also, her scent is all over me."
I couldn't believe what I was hearing. Seth was... boasting about me. I turned to face him. His deadly glare was locked onto the Overlord. A hand on my shoulder caused me to jump and squeak.
Seth's attention immediately diverted to me.

"Ha, little mutt got his voice back, and he's falling in love with the elemental," the Overlord laughed.

Ra cleared his throat and turned me to face him. "My dear Iris, I do apologize. No one knew your name until now. Well I mean I told Seth right before we went to fetch you, but that's all."

My lips parted. "M-my name is Iris?" I smiled and wrapped my arms around Ra, squeezing gently.

He returned the smile and gave me a quick hug before releasing me, likely due to Seth's growling.

"Yes, dear, you have a name. Why do you ask? Did you not know it?" he asked.

I shook my head and stepped back. "I don't remember much since waking up here in that cage. Besides a few times when I was moved around." I sighed. How much of my life here had I lost?

The Overlord groaned. "The elemental has a name, but you'll always be tainted!"

Anxiety flooded my heart, causing me to shake. It was embarrassing enough knowing that this man even had the opportunity to touch me and mock me. I couldn't help but feel powerless against him.

Chin up, Iris. Don't let this sack of skin belittle you.
Okay. This is going to sound silly.

I mustered up the courage as I addressed him; "You can poke fun at me all you want, Overlord, but what kind of name is 'Overlord'? This isn't *Guardians of the Galaxy*." I rolled my eyes as I began firing off insults. "You may have touched my outer layer, but Seth has touched more of me than you've ever touched any woman." I stomped up to the Overlord and raised my arm to slap him.

"Touch me and you'll be served to the Soulless on a gold platter, head-first," the Overlord warned.

"You touch her and I'll have a field day with you before I rip you apart," Seth threatened.

Ra sighed and pulled me away from the two as Seth approached the Overlord. The two stood staring each other down. "Iris, if you'd be so kind to join me over here to discuss what's going on so you can get caught up, we will let the boys do what they do best." he ushered me off to the side.

"But what about Seth? Is he going to be okay?" I turned to watch as the two of them stood unwavering.

"My dear, Seth is the God of Chaos. Nothing scares him… Except losing you, it seems," Ra smiled.

My eyes went wide. "Really?" I felt as if my ears were playing tricks on me. Did I just hear Ra, God of the sun and creation, tell me the God of Chaos was scared to lose... me?

"It's true. At the beginning of his search, he was always complaining about how he'd dump you off on the next guard once he found you, or how he'd leave you to die amongst the soulless." He calmly clasped his hands together in front of him and watched as Seth and the Overlord exchanged blows with one another.

"He said that, did he?" I narrowed my eyes at Seth, who was throwing a knee into the Overlord's gut.

"Well, as time went on and he felt you nearby, he began to worry that he was too late. When he doesn't speak, he's usually chatting non-stop in my head. He had me continually check the universe to make sure you were still alive. The only issue is, I couldn't locate you, since you're not from this timeline. But I could feel your life force," he explained.

"How long did he search for me?" I asked. My heart fluttered knowing Seth's dedication to his orders to find me. I thought back to the other guardian whose harsh voice I had heard when I was brought here, and what he had said earlier, and I smiled.

"Twelve years," Ra stated.
"Twelve years. That would make me forty-two... but the last thing I remember was sitting on the beach, and there was a--"
"Tsunami, yes. You succeeded in leveling the wave, but when you did that, you were pulled into a portal and brought here. You were being held by the creators of this chaos, and you slept for twelve years until Seth was close enough to trigger your awakening." Ra grimaced at the memory. "Unfortunately, the moment you woke up, the Soulless had homed in on your location as well."

"Ra, thank you for filling me in on the series of events which led up to today. But what happened to the world?" I gripped the sides of my dress, and watched Seth take a blow to the chest.

Seth stumbled back, his teeth bared. He seemed uninjured, though his shirt was torn in multiple places and his hair disheveled. I shook my head at him and watched as the Overlord attempted to pull a dagger from his belt. I rolled my eyes and twirled my finger. A pool of water formed under the Overlord's feet as he attempted to charge at Seth, only to land on the floor face first with a loud thud.

I brought my hand to my mouth and chuckled. Seth and Ra both turned to me.

Did you just...?

Yes, I did. Is there a problem?

The look on Seth's face struck fear in me. My hands went numb, and the tip of my nose was ice cold.

"Seth, stop that." Ra's voice pulled me from his trance.

He scoffed and walked over to the Overlord, who was still on the floor, groaning in pain holding his bleeding nose. Seth knelt in front of him and leaned into his ear something I was unable to hear.

"You're really going to go that far, for her?" the Overlord shouted while Seth grabbed him by the collar of his shirt and dragged him over to where I stood.

"Apologize to her," Seth ordered.

The Overlord snickered. "Only in your wildest dreams, Seth."

"Oh, goody. You're about to make his actual dream come true, then," I lied as I bounced on my toes, waiting for Seth's reaction.

Stop that.

I smirked. *Stop what?*

The bouncing... Your... Seth's eyes diverted to my chest.

You're such a man. I wouldn't expect anything less. I rolled my eyes and folded my arms across my chest.

"Wait, what do you mean his actual dream?" the Overlord's voice squeaked.

"Well, he's had a hard-on for ripping you apart since you did something unforgivable." I shrugged my shoulders. I thought back to earlier this morning, the lack of morality and sense of duty. He had no remorse for those he'd killed to save me.

The Overlord's eyes widened as he lifted his head. "What? You're kidding me. Killing me will change the timeline, and you know it."

"But an accidental death wouldn't," Seth commented before he slammed his foot into the Overlord's side, ejecting him across the room and into a granite column. His body hit the floor with a loud smack.

Painful groans echoed throughout the foyer. I gasped, pressing my hand to my lips. Seth wouldn't jeopardize the timeline, would he? Something profound inside of me was begging to stop him, but I couldn't will my legs to move.

"Did you kill him?" I asked with a shaky voice.

Seth looks at me with narrowed eyes. "Why do you care if I kill him or not? I thought you didn't want him around, either."

I turned my gaze from the Overlord to Seth. "I may not want him around, but you heard what that idiot said. Killing him would change the timeline." My volume crept upward into a shout. "It would drag us into one that neither of us have been to, so we have no idea how bad it is there compared to the one we're currently in!"

"You are such an indecisive woman. If you even think about saving him, you'll be next," Seth growled as he stomped off towards the Overlord.

I scoffed and turned to walk out of the building. "You can't hurt me!" I shouted once more. "You know what? I don't have time to argue with you. I'm leaving."

"You'll be back. Take all the time you need, Miss Iris. We will be waiting. Well, Seth will probably follow after you!" Ra shouted as I searched for another exit.

"This is going to be more difficult than I thought." I sighed as I made my way to what I assumed was the exit.

"Where do you think you're going?" came a voice from behind me.

I turned around at the familiar voice. Was this the guard from before? "I'm going out for air. Is there something wrong with that?" I shot back.

"You were ordered to stay here." The man brought his visor up, revealing a pale face and bright red eyes. He wore the same outfit as Seth but with fewer guns and more knives. The man smirked, revealing fangs that stretched down to his bottom lip.

This one must be a vampire. What is he doing awake and in the sun? Surely he would be dead. I placed a hand on my hip and cocked my head. "I wasn't told to do anything, and if I remember correctly, you aren't in charge of me." I turned around again and continued to leave.

A low hiss escaped the man's lips. "Don't walk away from me when I'm talking to you!"

I stopped and rolled my eyes. The guardians' demands were becoming more and more annoying by the second. "I will do what I want when I want to," I retorted.

I was pulled back by an unseen force. The man appeared in front of me. His hand gripped my forearm with bruising pressure. The fire in his eyes danced as his gaze locked onto mine.

"You are a stubborn woman, aren't you? Why don't you listen like the others and learn your place?" he growled.

The bile in my stomach jumped to my chest.

Why do you seem to keep disappearing? Seth sounded bemused.

I snorted. *Because I'm fucking pissed off.*

That's unfortunate, he admitted. *But you have no idea who's out there right now.*

Oh, now you fucking care.

Don't do that. You already know I don't have a choice.

I resisted the urge to growl audibly. *Fuck you, Seth.*

Gladly. Maybe you'd calm the fuck down if I actually did, he replied, annoyed.

That was an insult, not an offer.

The man's grip tightened. I cried out in pain as I struggled to pull free. "Let me go, now!" I shouted, only for him to slam my back against the wall.

I moaned in pain as the back of my head bounced off the granite. I locked eyes with the guard, a scowl on my face. "Let me go, now," I warned.

He leaned in dangerously close to my neck. The tip of his fang grazed over my jugular. "No. As a matter of fact, you're coming with me. I'd rather not have to hunt for my next meal," he snarled. He brought his hand to my throat and clasped it tightly.

I grabbed his hand and drove my nails into his skin, eliciting a hiss. With the fluid in his own body, I constricted his arm, and he began to shout obscenities.

"You fucking bitch!" He raised his free hand to strike me, only to stop at the sound of a voice that echoed down the empty hallway.

"I'd let her go if I were you, Kelvin." Ra's voice echoed from the end of the hallway.
Kelvin quickly turned his head to face the sound, only to find no one there. "Who the hell?" he whispered, releasing his hold on my throat.
"See, you remember the man who brought me here?" I gasped for air.

"The one who doesn't speak? Yeah, what about him?" he replied.
"Well he does now…" I sang off key as I turned my head to watch a shirtless Seth drop the Overlord's bloodied and unconscious body on the ground and charge at Kelvin.
Seth cranked his arm back and launched it at him. His fist made contact with Kelvin's chest, sending him crashing through the double doors at the end of the hall. He then turned to me, anger filling his eyes.

"What the hell were you thinking?" he yelled.
I turned my gaze to the floor and rubbed the bruise on my arm, hoping to conceal it from him. "I had it under control."
"Except you didn't," he yelled once more. He grabbed my arm to examine the bruise. "Do you even know what he could have done to you? Are you going to be a pain in my ass and run around thinking you

can handle everything?" He slammed his fist into the wall next to my head, causing me to flinch. My heart jumped into my throat as I shook.

"Stop fucking yelling at me! I am a woman, not a porcelain doll. I am not easily broken. You--" I shook my head as tears brimmed in my eyes. "I--I can't do this right now. This is too much for one day." I maneuvered around him and took off running down the hallway, hopping over Kelvin's limp body and into the sunlight. I didn't stop for a breath as my sadness and anxiety became erratic and completely irrational. I had no idea where I was headed when I finally decided to stop by a small pond.

As tears poured from my eyes, a sweet and gentle voice called out to me. "Oh my dear, what's wrong? Why are you crying?" the voice asked.

I looked up to see a naked... Nymph? The woman's skin was a dull shade of blue and smooth, her hair flowing with the breeze. Her eyes were a pale gray, but her lips were soft pink. I blinked a few times while wiping my spilled tears. "I--I'm okay. Things are just a little... rough today."

"Well, you can talk to us if you need to. We're all in this together." She placed her hand on mine. "What's your name, sweetheart?"

I give her a small smile. "I'm Iris."

Her jaw and the ground met as her eyes widened. "Th-the Iris? The legendary Iris? The one who is supposed to give Mother Earth back her life?" Her eyes began to water.

A few ladies surfaced from the pond's depths. Their looks mirrored the woman in front of me.

"Wait, are you really her?"

"I thought she was a myth!"

"Wait, did you just say that woman is Iris?" another woman's voice called from a distance.

I turned to face the sound and was surprised to see a pack of large wolves and what I assumed was a pixie. She had looked exactly how they were described in my old college course on Mythical Anthropology class. Her red curls framed her tiny, freckled face.

"It *is* her! Oh, wonderful!" the pixie squealed, flying over to me. She hugged my cheek with her tiny hands. The rapid fluttering of her iridescent wings tickled my skin, causing me to giggle, and I hugged her with a cupped hand in return.

The wolves surrounded us, lay down in what seemed to be a protective formation, and released a howl that slowly pulled the sun from day to sunset. I awed at the sight.

"It's beautiful," I whispered, staring at the sunset. The sky was painted in beautiful shades of purple, orange, and pink. On the west side of the Dome just below the tree line, the moon peeked above the horizon.

My heart melted. I knelt on the grass in front of the pond and smiled at the others. "This place is beautiful compared to the other side of the Dome. What happened? All I know is that there was a war."

The nymphs turned their gazes to the water. The little pixie twiddled her thumbs as she made her way back over to a large, red-furred wolf, and the other wolves became visibly uncomfortable. An overwhelming sense of dread filled my veins.

The largest of the wolves sighed loudly before rising from her spot on the grass and approached me. Her fur was black and her eyes gold. "Do you really want to know?" she asked.

I nodded only to see her head fall. "Twelve years ago, the world's government became greedy. Their greed led to the discovery of our people. The myths and legends of our existence pushed their curiosity. Someone revealed to them that they needed to build or create some sort of weapon to pull us out of our human cloaks so they could--"

"Cyrus," one of the pack members chided. "That's not our story to tell. Maybe let Seth do it."

"She will know in due time, but right now I can't afford to overload her brain. She's already used her ability three times today. Her loss of energy is taking a toll on her." Seth's voice came from behind me.

The hairs on the back of my neck stood rigid. I gulped in fear that Seth was still upset with me. I shut my eyes, placing my head in my hands. My temples were beginning to throb.

The sound of grass shifting told me that everyone had moved out of Seth's way when he approached me.

"Is that why I feel so irrational? Scared? Exhausted? I can't think, and I feel like I'm going crazy," I whimpered, the throbbing pulsed in my temples.
    "That's exactly why. Your energy field is low. You over-exerted yourself." Seth's voice was soothing as he scooped me up. "You all can visit later. Iris needs to rest."
    I gripped onto his arm weakly and rested my head against his chest. "Sorry for ruining the day," I said. The pain in my head pulled the breath from my lungs.
    With that, we dropped into another portal and appeared in the living room of Seth's tiny home. He carried me into the spare bedroom with ease and set me down on the bed.
    "You need to eat," Seth stated, already on his way through the door. In a few moments, he returned with a bowl of fruit and a glass of red liquid.

"I don't think I can eat anything," I whispered. "My head hurts so much right now I can't even think."
    The bed shifted, and I spun to see Seth sitting behind me after placing the glass and bowl on the nightstand. He opened his arms and urged me to come forward. I hesitated for a moment, part of me wary of his intentions, but eventually I scooted closer to him and leaned into his embrace.

Wrapping his arms around me, he lay back on the headboard and pressed my head to his chest. "Just relax," he cooed, touching his hand to my forehead.

The pain melted away to nothing, and I could finally breathe. As exhaustion overcame me, the adrenaline in my system finally faded. I placed my hand over my mouth to stifle a yawn.

"Do you want to get cleaned up before you fall asleep?" Seth asked.

"No, I just showered. I don't think I need to until the morning. I'm so--" Without even finishing my sentence, I drifted off to sleep.

Chapter 8: Count Down

Ian

With a cigarette in my hand, I watched as my machines whirled around in overtime to prepare the first set of clones. The facility was one of many I had stationed around this desecrated land in Florida.

This wasn't the best of hiding spots, as Florida was mainly flat land, too close to the shores. Knowing that woman had the ability to wield the element of water, I wasn't comfortable keeping everyone here.

Bringing my hand to my mouth, I caught the filter between my lips and sucked the harsh nicotine into my lungs.

"Oh, what a wonderful sight to see." I exhaled the smoke and smiled when the rows of incubators fell in place. These adults were coming to life and their bodies twitched.

My pocket buzzed with an annoying ringing tone. I reached into the pouch and grabbed my phone. My face lit up as I read the name displayed across the screen. I smiled as I hit the green acceptance button and then placed the phone on the speaker setting.

"My, my, I'm glad to hear back from you. What's going on?"

"You wouldn't believe what this piece of— "

"But I would believe. This is Seth we are talking about here. What did he do? Is my clone still standing, or did he finally perish?"

The man on the line scoffed. "He's alive. But not for long. Seth and Iris are going to kill him."

"And what is it you want from me?"

"I want to make a deal."

"You have my interest. What deal would you like to make? Unless you're doing this out of pure survival, which itself would be humorous to me. You are a God after all, are you not?"

"Listen, Ian. You should know better than to speak to me in that fashion," the man growled.

"Oh, but weren't you using this weird lingo not too long ago? Now isn't the time to be proper. Anywho…"

"I need more power. And I know you can give me that."

"Then bring me the girl and kill Seth. Simple. Once this is all over, these beings will fall to their knees awaiting your rule, but I would prefer it if you killed them." I smirked, taking another drag from my cigarette before dropping it to the floor, and stomping it out.

"The girl has a name," he ground out.

"Oh? Do tell. That was one thing I wasn't able to figure out. Even in the twelve years she was with me."

"It's Iris. Her name is Iris."

"Oh? What a beautiful name for a beautiful specimen," I chuckled.

"I'll bring her to you and do your dirty work if you keep your word," he huffed.

"I am going to need one more thing from you."

The man on the other side groaned. "What?"

A smirk played across my lips. "I need that book… the black book."

"Consider it done," the man stated before the line disconnected.

I clasped my hands together as my plan had now been put into motion. These filthy creatures would finally perish, if they were not enslaved.

-A millennium prior-

"How is it that you seem to keep disappearing to other planets, nephew?" came a voice from behind me.

I raised a brow and turned to face the man. "I don't have the slightest clue as to what you mean."

The man clenched his feathery hand. "You know exactly what I mean. You just left Pluto. The cold planet is now ashes floating amongst space. How much more are you going to destroy?" he sneered.

Clasping my hands together, I shrugged. "As many as I need to until I find what I'm looking for: power."

"Atlas. Just get rid of him. If he has no plans to turn from this path of destruction, we need to handle him now. You need to make sure you keep track of where the universe sends him next," said voice from the abyss as the darkness engulfed me.

Who am I?

The scene before me shifted to a raging fire atop a familiar hill. My eyes widened at the realization that this was my family home. I gripped the sides of my head and let out a scream, and I fell to my knees.

Darkened silhouettes of what looked like giant birds took to the skies, their claws gripping some sort of bag as they disappeared into the night.

Present Day

I snapped out of my thoughts for a moment. *These memories aren't mine. Why does that wretched abomination keep calling me his nephew?*

I clenched my fist and turned to leave the facility, knowing that my inside man would get me the final item I needed for these clones. I stopped short of the door and grabbed a tablet from its stationed spot on the wall and opened the timed release.

"Shouldn't be too long. Let's set it for a year to give these pure souls some time to adjust to their new bodies," I mumbled to myself as I fiddled with the device and hit the countdown switch before setting it back in its place.

"Soon... Everything will be mine."

Chapter 9: Forbidden Fruit

Seth

I let out a long breath and looked down at Iris. From what I could tell, she had fallen asleep. *This woman is going to be the death of me.* I chuckled at the thought.

Make sure the Overlord is still restrained, I sent. *I'll take care of him in the morning.*

And why can't you finish him off right now?

I'm sort of in a predicament.

The curiosity behind the transmission blossomed into full-blown nosiness. *Oh? Do tell.*
Iris is asleep.
Perfect. She wo—
On my chest.
Oh, my man! Ha!
Osiris, I'd prefer if you didn't use weird lingo…

Except you've been cussing more and using this weird lingo that you seem to have picked up from those humans.

Can you please stop with the bullshit?

Fine, fine. I'll make sure he's still in the cage. I can't promise he won't have any additional broken bones, though.

A smile quirked at the edge of my lips. *That's fine. Goodnight.*

I pulled the blanket back on the empty side of the bed and carefully moved Iris over, only for her grip on my arm to tighten.

"Don't go, please," she begged weakly.

I placed my hand on hers, squeezing gently. "I won't. But I do need to change my clothes... and yours." I whispered, glancing at her dress, which was less-than-ideal for sleeping.

Iris lazily stood up and stripped her off her dress in one go, then plopped down onto the mattress and pulled the covers over her nakedness. I didn't know what to think or what to do besides try my best to ignore the lustful thoughts zooming around in my mind. I felt myself come alive in my pants, causing me to groan.

I stealthily rolled off the bed and out of her room and over to mine right next door where I stripped my clothes off quickly. I caught a glimpse of myself in the mirror and paused. "What the hell," I said in a low voice as I moved closer to examine my skin.

I flipped the light switch on to get a better look and found my chest and torso covered in what looked like ancient Egyptian scripture. 'From guardian to destiny, one must follow the path. Love is anything but ordinary.'

I pinched the bridge of my nose and sighed heavily. "Asherah, what do I have to do? Why did you stick me with this duty? Protection is one thing, but love? You really think someone like me is capable of love?" I sneered.

"You're completely capable of love, and you know it. But you know it opens you up to being vulnerable, and you don't like that." came Asherah's voice from beside me.

"But why me?" I asked. "Surely you could have assigned someone else to do this."

Asherah chuckled. "Because you're the only one who has the power she needs in order to revive Mother Earth to her natural form, and from what I've witnessed, you've taken a liking to this one."

So, this is what love feels like? My heart fluttering in my chest, the yearning for the warmth of her skin against mine? I shook my head and turned around, only to find that Asherah had disappeared, just like she had twelve years ago.

I sighed loudly, grabbed a pair of sweatpants and a simple T-shirt, and left my room to find Iris standing between the rooms clutching only a sheet. The curve of her ass peeked out from behind it.

"Iris, what are you doing out of bed?" I raised a brow.

She didn't respond, and I crouched down to her level and waved my hand in front of her face, only to notice that her eyes were closed.

"Iris? Hello?" I tapped the tip of her nose.

Iris's eyes flew open.

"What happened? Why am I naked?" She grabbed the sheet and wrapped it around herself with haste. "Seth, what did you do to me?" Fear laced her tone.

"I didn't do anything! I told you I was going to change and come back since you wanted me to stay with you tonight. You tore your dress off then went back to sleep," I explained.

"Then why do I hurt everywhere?" She sniffled.

"What?" I looked at the floor and saw a small pool of red liquid spreading around her feet. I lifted her quickly and moved her back to my room. I placed her on the California-king-sized bed and pulled the sheet off of her.

I scanned her from head to toe, ignoring her curves and my own temptations for her sake. After seeing no signs of injury, I finally noticed the red stain starting from between her breasts trailing down to her feet. "Did you grab that glass from the nightstand?" I asked.

"I don't remember," she replied weakly, rubbing the sleep from her eyes.

I quickly covered her with the sheet and ran to her room. Indeed, the glass lay spilled, exactly as I expected. Iris must have reached for it and accidentally spilled it on herself. The satin sheet collected it, then dumped it the moment she stood up.

I walked back to my room to find Iris curled into a ball in the middle of my bed, wrapped in the sheet. I placed my hands on my hips and stared at her sleeping figure for a moment. "It's not like I sleep, anyway," I grumbled to myself before shuffling over to the edge of the bed. I reached down and lifted the blanket to slide over her as I sat down.

"Asherah, you'd better be right about this, or I'll have to escort you to the scales myself," I whispered as I lay down, closing my eyes.

A few hours went by, and I couldn't seem to fall asleep. I tossed and turned without waking Iris. I couldn't imagine how worn out she was, even though she had slept for those twelve years.

Osiris, are you awake? I asked.

Do I ever sleep when the world is in peril?

Good point.
What do you need at such an ungodly hour?
Uh, nothing, I was just checking—
It's about the girl, isn't it?
I hesitated for a moment as I looked over at Iris. *Yes...*
Well, speak.

When you met Isis, how did you know you, erm... the L-word...

Love? Osiris seemed flabbergasted at the question. *How did I know?*

It's challenging to explain... Did your heart ever betray you and everything you stood for? Did you feel an overwhelming pressure to protect and defend her without being ordered to?

I felt a smirk across our connection. *Well, that's one way to describe it.*

Did you feel calm, yet frustrated?
I did. Is that what you're feeling for the girl?
I hesitated for a moment, searching. *It seems that way.*
Asherah set you up.

I sat upright. *What do you mean?*

69

That... You'll get that explanation later. For right now, you need to figure out your feelings before you do something rash. Or I decide to take her from you.

You wouldn't dare.
I took Nephthys from you, didn't I?
You can definitely fuck off now.

Hey, don't hate the player, hate the game, as the humans used to say.

I flopped back on the pillow again, an aggravated huff escaping my lips. *I should kill you... Again. You are no help at all.*

Hey, that's what I'm here for—to make sure your life is just the right amount of difficult, ha! Goodnight!

What a waste of time, I thought to myself as I rolled over on my side. I propped my head on my pillow and watched Iris sleep. Her head was tucked away in the buffer, and her body was still wrapped like a burrito in the sheets. I had a strong desire to touch her skin. I gently pulled at the sheet in search of her arm, only to find it tucked under the pillow as well.

I moved her arm from under the pillow and placed it beside her, causing her to stir. I smiled at her sleepy moans and gently ran the tips of my fingers along her arm and her exposed upper back. The warmth radiating from her gave me comfort. Suddenly, she pulled the sheet from under her and wrapped her leg around my hips as she moved closer to me, resting her head on my chest.

My cheeks flushed with heat, and I swear I could feel myself becoming aroused by this gesture. *What the hell was I thinking? I can't take this too far.* I placed my hand on her head, only to discover how soft her hair was. A sense of longing came over me, and I ran my fingers through her hair.

She stirred, looking up at me with sleepy eyes. "Seth, what are you doing?" she asked sleepily.

"I could ask you the same thing." I jutted my chin in the direction of where her leg was and scoffed.

Embarrassed, she pushed herself off of me quickly. "Don't tell me we—"

I shook my head. "No, I wouldn't do that without your consent. I'm not the Overlord. I can handle my temptations... For now. You, on the other hand, I can't be so sure of."

Her cheeks flushed a shade of red. I could tell she was getting flustered at the situation. I pointed to her nakedness and chuckled. "Did you forget something?"

She quickly looked down and then back at me with a horrified look on her face. "Why, you pervert!" She grabbed the sheet and pulled it over her exposed skin.

"Hey, you're the one who stripped in front of me. I didn't undress you." I shrugged. "But you should get cleaned up. You tried to drink that elixir I gave you earlier and managed to spill it on yourself."

"Is that why I feel sticky?" she asked.

"Yes," I replied. "I didn't want to disturb you, so I didn't clean you up."

Why did I say that? I internally screamed. It had indeed been challenging to hold back my urges to be near her at all times. When I couldn't see her, I got jittery and nervous. My brain went into overdrive, and I just wanted her close.

"Did you just say--"

"Yes, you heard what you heard. I'm not going to repeat it," I retorted.

Iris moved closer to me and wrapped her arms around my neck, embracing me. "Thank you for being considerate."

My heart raced, my mind flooding with feelings I couldn't describe. Again, I was left speechless. I wrapped my arms around Iris, squeezing her gently. Her warmth clouded my mind. Instinctively, I leaned down and kissed the top of her head, then pulled away to rest against the headboard.

71

To my surprise, Iris looked up at me and smiled. We stared at each other for a moment. I froze, wondering what she was thinking. As if my body had a mind of its own, one hand snaked around her waist. I pulled her closer as I slid the other hand behind her neck.

Iris didn't resist my touch, and I welcomed her as she placed her hands on my chest.

Our gazes never shifting, I pressed my forehead to hers and closed my eyes for a moment... Only to open them a split second later when Iris pressed her lips against mine. Sparks ignited into a flame, and a sense of urgency washed over me. I pulled Iris onto my lap as our lips danced passionately.

The taste of honey on her lips was one to savor. My hands roamed her body, and hers explored mine. I sensed her core burning with a need that I wasn't sure I was ready to satisfy.

"Iris," I panted, "we can't." Disappointment and sadness radiated from her as I broke the kiss. Our chests heaved with deep breaths.

"But why not?" Her lower lip extended in a pout.

"Because you're not in your right mind. I don't want you to do something you'll regret." I let out a long breath to slow my racing heart. As those words left my lips, she shifted her gaze to the bed.

"I don't know what I want, but I do know that this fire burning inside of me can only be extinguished by you. You proved that earlier today." She sighed, pulled away from me, and slid to the edge of the bed, clutching the sheet.

"Wait, are you in pain now? Did I—shit, what did I do?" I ran my hand through my hair.

"I'm always in pain when I'm close to you. It's strange, really, the way my body responds to you. It's like we've known each other for the better part of eternity, but I just met you..." she whispered.

"Then let me take away that pain. I promise not to go too far." I pulled my shirt off and positioned myself behind her. Leaning into the crook of her neck, I kissed the exposed skin behind her ear. She replied with a gasp and a light moan as she leaned into me. With one hand between her thighs and the other cupping her breast I whispered into her ear, "Lean back and relax. I'll take it from here."

Iris arched her back and tilted her head up at me. Her breathing picked up when I slid two fingers into her, and rubbed her bud with my thumb. She purred with delight as she grabbed my hand and let out a low moan.

I pulled her back onto the bed and held her close. She rode out her climax. I showered her in light kisses while she caught her breath. She kept her eyes closed and curled into me.

"Sleep tight, little one," I whispered while I pulled the sheet over her and drifted off to sleep.

Chapter 10: Revealed Feelings

Iris

I woke to the shifting of the bed. I tried to sit up, only to be pulled back by something bulky around my waist, and a comforting warmth flushed against my back. The heat in my cheeks rose as I felt around for a moment and realized that this object was indeed Seth's arm, and the warmth was his bare torso against my naked back.

"Oh dear," I whispered and attempted to sit up once again, only for him to pull me closer. His erection rubbed against my thigh, which made me squeak.

Seth playfully ground his hips against my backside. "Where are you going?" he mumbled sleepily.

"Um, to pee?" I replied.

He groaned. "Just a little longer?"

"But I have to *pee*," I whined, removing his arm from around me. I jumped up and darted into the bathroom to relieve myself, then promptly washed away the sticky elixir off. After exiting the bathroom, I reached to grab my hair, then realized with a downward glance that I was still naked. I quickly tiptoed into my room and searched the drawers for something suitable. A quick glance out the window told me that the sun hadn't risen yet, so I needed pajamas.

"What are you doing?" Seth called out to me.

"Uh, I needed something to wear…" I replied.

He chuckled. "It's obvious I've already seen you naked."

I rolled my eyes and snatched a robe hanging beside the standing mirror on my way back to his room.

I crawled back into bed and pulled the covers over my head without looking at Seth. My mind replayed the events from just a few hours before, causing my core to tingle.

"Oh no, not again," I groaned.

"What's wrong?" Quick as lightning, Seth turned to me and pulled the covers down.

"Just the thought... of what we did. Well what you did," I whispered.

Seth raised his brow at me. "You really are insatiable aren't you?"

"It's not funny... It really isn't!" I snapped.

"Does it look like I'm laughing?" He narrowed his eyes at me, causing me to tuck my head into the pillow.

"Why won't this feeling go away, Seth?" I whimpered.

Seth slipped his arms around my waist and pulled me closer to him. I tucked my face into his chest and squeezed my thighs together, hoping that would help ease the tingling sensation.

Seth took in a deep breath and exhaled slowly. "I don't know why you're like this, but your arousal is going to push me over the edge. Unless you want that... But I can't guarantee I'll be able to stop myself. I need to know if this is what you want, or if you want me to use another method."

I began to shake. The thought of the pain I would be subjected to at random times if I didn't undo the Overlord's magic, versus the pain I might endure giving up this body's virginity, caused my anxiety to flare. "Why couldn't I bring my old body to this timeline? Surely this wouldn't have been a problem," I mumbled. I couldn't imagine it being worse than this. I'd been in pain before, but it'd never been this excruciating, and at this point, over the last few hours, it had become unbearable.

"Why me?" I whispered, shifting my gaze up at his face. "Why did she choose me? Why does Mother God need me? Of all of the spirituals in the world, Mother God chose me." My bottom lip quivered.

Seth softened his gaze and pressed his lips to my forehead. "Because she knew you were strong enough to handle any obstacle thrown your way. You've never given up. Hell, you've asked for quite a few favors over the years, and she knows you'd be able to put up with my grouchy attitude."

"What do you mean by that? Your attitude?" I asked.

He smiled. "I don't necessarily like people." He trailed off for a moment. "Even in this short period of time I've come to the realization that the only person I need is—" He stopped abruptly and paused for a moment, his cheeks turning a darker shade of red.

"Oh, did I miss something? You've been alive since the beginning of time. How long has it been since you've loved a woman?" I coughed.

Seth sighed once more. His muscles tensed around me as he shifted uncomfortably. "See, I did once, and she was taken from me. A soul refused to take the path leading to the scales, and she…"

I placed my hand on his chest. "Don't. You don't have to explain. I get it." I thought back to my husband, my children. Though I'd been ripped from them, it felt like they'd been taken from me in equal measure. Indeed, I understood his pain perfectly.

"That's the thing. You understand that with life comes death: the thing most people wouldn't dare to understand. Hell, you've even gotten me to hold a conversation. You know I don't speak much, but with you, everything flows like it's supposed to. It's strange. I feel a sense of calm with you. I feel— hell, this is a funny way to put it, but... Alive. I can't bear to see you sad or in pain, but sometimes you're a pain in the ass." He booped the tip of my nose, causing me to blink in confusion.

"So, what you're saying is, after twelve years of hopelessly searching for me, you came to love who I was, regardless of what I looked like, only because I understood you better than the previous women in your life? I assume there's been more than just me. Besides your--"

"You would be the second ever in my life," he cut in, squeezing me gently. "And you'll be the last."

"But my time is limited here on Earth, as is everyone else's in the Dome. We are mortals. What could possibly keep me alive long enough to spend eternity with a man I just met?" I recoiled.

"Your soul. It'll be mine. I guarantee it." He smiled, bringing his face closer to mine as he lifted my chin.

The creaking of the floorboards in the doorway alarmed both of us. Seth pulled away from me quickly and shifted his attention to the intruder.

"Oh, it smells like you two had fun in here." said an unfamiliar voice sounded from the doorway, causing Seth to quickly jump up, pushing me behind him.

"Oh, dear brother, relax. It's just me," it said.

I peeked from behind Seth to see a man in a blue dress shirt and black slacks leaning against the door frame. "Who are you?" I asked.

"Did you not just hear me? I'm Seth's brother, Osiris," he sneered.

Seth's muscles tensed. "You should have told me you were coming."

Osiris shrugged. "And ruin the special moment you and Miss Iris were having? I think not."

"Well, you ruined it either way," I grumbled.

"Oh dear child, I'd watch your mouth if I were you. There are plenty of soulless hunting you now that you're awake. Speaking of which, have you two—" He pointed to both of us, his eyebrows wiggling.

"No," Seth answered simply.

"Then why does it smell like you did? C'mon, Seth, you don't have to lie." Osiris laughed, his gaze toward me shifted into one of lust as he bit his lower lip seductively.

All I could do was keep quiet. My cheeks were hot to the touch. This encounter was way too embarrassing to deal with, especially with multiple people knowing about my problem.

Seth narrowed his eyes and stepped out of the room, pushing Osiris out with him. He took one look at me with a softened expression before closing the door.

I internally screamed. *What the hell was that all about?* I thought. Being an intact female was difficult enough. *Maybe I should take care of it myself... What if it hurts more? Why the hell am I so confused about all of this?* I held my head in my hands and shook.

Seth's voice rumbled in my mind. *There's a small door beside the bed that leads to your room. I closed the door for you if you want to get dressed.* After a pause, he continued, *Don't wear a dress today.*

Why?
Because you still need to shower. All the men in the Dome can smell your unique scent, especially the wolves.
I let out a groan. *That's comforting.*
Seth replied with a low growl.
It was a joke. I smiled. *I'm just going to shower now, get dressed, and then lie back down a bit longer.*
You're never going to listen, huh?
My smile spread into a grin. *Not a chance in hell.*
I slowly rose from the bed and tiptoed to the main door, pressing my ear against it. I tried to make out Seth and Osiris' conversation. So far, it seemed as if Seth was extremely upset about his brother's untimely arrival.
"What do you mean she's always in pain? I thought she had a family in the other timeline? Did someone get to her before you did?" Osiris shouted.
"Not necessarily," Seth replied.
"Elaborate."

"When I first brought her here, the Overlord did something. He mentioned something about her abilities being locked away, but he got her worked up. But from what I can tell, the moment I found her, something awakened. The only issue is, I don't know how to fucking unlock her other abilities." The sound of glass breaking caused me to gasp and flinch from behind the door.

"Then you know what you have to do, Seth, for your sake and hers. Don't keep her waiting too long. She's not going to be able to focus today. If anything, I can do it instead of you."

Seth released a possessive growl. "You will do no such thing." He paused for a moment. "What the hell is going on today? We had nothing planned that I knew of."

"Ra wants you to help her with managing her energy and get some practice in with her two abilities, and you still need to cause a scene."

"If I— we do this... Will that take away her pain? I'm only concerned about that right now."

"Her pain isn't even from the fact that she's craving; it's from the fact that the Overlord tied her abilities, and they are wanting to be released. Anyway, that's what I've heard. You two getting down and dirty should untie her other abilities. I can't guarantee it, Seth. But you'll be soul-bound to her, so be careful."

I took a deep breath at the conversation and straightened my posture before throwing the door open. I marched out and headed straight for the bathroom without even glancing at Seth. From the energy he was emitting, I could feel his anger, confusion, and pain. His emotions stabbed through me.

I slammed the bathroom door and pressed my back against the wood. I was scared. Scared to make Seth wait for me and even then, how could I go through with this? The Overlord had tied my abilities? The pain I felt couldn't be nearly as bad as what he was going through. I felt like I'd been unknowingly punishing a man who had put my needs, safety, and life before his own.

I pulled my robe off and tossed it to the floor as I walked over to the shower and turned it on. I waited for a moment as I tested the water before jumping in. "Today is going to be a better day. Today is going to be a better day," I chanted to myself in a low voice.

I stepped under the hot stream and let out a sigh of satisfaction as my aching muscles released their tension. "This feels amazing... It's almost better than sex."

How would you know? You've never done it. Not in this timeline anyways. He sent me.

Oh, shut up. How could one forget the feeling...? A girl can dream.

Do you remember what that feeling is? He chuckled. *You know I can make that dream come true.*

His corny line made me roll my eyes. *Let's not do this right now. I'm enjoying myself.*

Oh, really? Seth pushed the images of our intimate moment through to me. The strokes of his fingers, his warmth enveloping me.

Stop that! You're going to start something with your brother present!

Oh, he's already gone, so with your permission we totally could start something. He chuckled again.

I really dislike you right now.
Ouch. My heart.
You don't have one right now.

Groaning, I rinsed myself off and jumped out of the shower. I reached for a towel off of the shelf to dry myself before tending to my hair. "I can make your dream come true," I mimicked in a whiny tone as I patted my hair dry and braided it. "Can't believe this whole ordeal."

I wrapped myself in another towel and opened the door, walking straight into my room only to find Seth holding two differently colored dresses.

"Ahem, what are you doing?" I asked. "Didn't you say no dresses?"

Seth glanced at me, then back to the dresses. "I was trying to help you make a decision on clothing today, but I think this one will do. I'm not so sure you're ready for combat boots and gear." He handed me a haltered sky-blue dress cut off below the knee with a matching pair of sandals and walked out of the room.

I couldn't help but grin at his sincerity as I picked up the dress and examined it further. "I am going to need something else," I muttered to myself. "Hmm, I thought I saw something in this drawer..." I pulled the drawer I was searching in earlier and found undergarments. Surprisingly, they were all my size. "So, where did you say you got all of these clothes again, Seth?" I shouted.

Asherah made everything. Funny thing is, she told me she had no idea what you looked like. But I think that was a lie, since everything is tailored to your body.

After sifting through the bunch, I found a pair of black spandex boy-shorts and slipped into them as I dropped my towel. "Oh, these are perfect!" I jumped with excitement. "Yep, kicking ass in a dress and sandals should be a breeze." I sang to myself as I slipped into the dress and unbraided my hair, but then decided to throw it into a messy bun. Taking a quick glance in the mirror, I left the room and headed back into Seth's room, only to walk in on him fast asleep, his shirtless form sprawled over the mattress.

During our time together, granted it hadn't been long, I never actually taken a good look at his body. Of course, with him being a God, it was expected for him to be sculpted. Rocking a six pack with a chiseled chest and arms, he also had thighs that could quickly drop-kick a building into submission. My gaze stopped at his groin, the print of his obvious erection showed, causing me to wonder.

Why is it that Gods are always packing? I huffed.

I stood staring and admiring his figure for a moment before my tummy grumbled. I pouted my lower lip and tiptoed into the kitchen. I found a bowl of fruit with a note beside it. "This will help you when the hunger sets in. Don't worry, hunger is only temporary in this timeline." Reading the note aloud, I smiled. "Well, don't mind if I do," I whispered, wiggling my hips in excitement. I grabbed an orange-colored spherical fruit and headed for the door.

I slowly pulled the door open, stepped out to the chilled night breeze and inhaled before closing the door behind me. "Oh, this is wonderful," I said with a low tone and headed for a hill not too far from Seth's little house.

The bright light of the moon guided me as I passed through the scarce foliage toward the hill. When the tall grass brushed against my skin, tiny sparks of light appeared, floating just above it as they drifted over to a nearby field. I stopped for a moment to watch in amazement.

"Oh my goodness, I haven't seen fireflies in forever!" I whispered excitedly.

"Then you'll love this," a voice sounded from beside me.

I quickly glanced over as a large gray wolf ran through the grass, causing the fireflies to scatter into the sky. Smiling to myself, I took in another deep breath before turning to face the wolf, who was making his way back. His yellow eyes glowed while they held their gaze on me.

"That was an amazing sight to see. Thank you." I nodded and continued my way to the hill with the wolf in tow.

"May I ask where you're going in the middle of the night?" the wolf asked.

"I just needed some air. Being cooped up with Seth is taking a toll on me," I sighed.

The pitter-patter of quick steps caused me to look down at the wolf as he appeared beside me. "What do you mean? Seth hasn't hurt you, has he?" His ears were laid back, his brow raised.

I shook my head. "No, no, nothing like that. It's just... I don't know how to explain it."

"Well, the sun will be up soon. Cyrus will be shifting it here shortly. I would head back if I were you," he said before disappearing into the tall grass.

I pressed my lips together, debating on turning around and going back to the house or going to the hilltop. "How mad could he be?" I shrugged and continued.

A little while later, I finally reached the top of the hill, and I turned to look back at the tiny village. "What a beautiful sight to see. Even in the dark," I muttered.

I quickly found a place to sit under a big tree with a lavender scent and gazed up at the sky. I took a bite of the fruit I'd snagged from the bowl at the house. The mixture of citrus and apple flavors was refreshing yet confusing with each bite. I pulled the fruit away and raised a brow. "Is this an orange or an apple? Wacky fruit."

"Psst, Iris. What are you doing up here? Especially in the middle of the night?" a voice called out to me.

I quickly searched the area for the source of the voice. "I uh, needed some air. Where are you?"

"Well, if you actually used your ears, you'd be able to hear that I am above you." She chuckled.

I shifted my gaze upward and gasped at the sight of a dark-winged creature as it leapt down from the branch above. "You... You're a— "

"Griffin? Yes, honey." A smile crept up the sides of her face. She sat on her hind legs as she landed beside me. Folding in her massive wings. Bright golden eyes matched her feathers and fur.

"The body of a lion, the head of a hawk, and the ears of an owl. You are such a beautiful being!" I squealed in excitement. "May I?" I reached out to her.

"Of course! Pets are always welcomed. I'm Phoebe. I used to be an accountant at a law firm, but of course we all know the tale of what happened." She extended her head in my direction.

I ran my hand across her feathers and let out a light breath. "You're so soft. It's comforting, really." Phoebe's golden feathers were as soft as silk.

"I know, they are quite something. Anyway, what are you doing out here alone? Are you handling the adjustment alright?" She began firing off questions.

"I just needed some air. Being near Seth right now is causing me more pain than anything. He's not hurting me, but this connection we have, it's strange really."

"How so?" She crossed her front paws and cocked her head.

"Well, internally my insides are constantly on fire. I don't know how to explain it."

Phoebe let out a squawk. "Please spare me the details. I know what you mean. My mate was killed in the war, so I know. I hope you don't mind me keeping you company in the meantime.

"I would love the company, but I don't know how Seth would react to you. Has he seen you before?"

Phoebe shrugged her shoulders, "I don't care if he has or hasn't. The maiden that's supposed to save us shouldn't be out here alone, especially with Kelvin running amuck. So I'm going to hang out until he comes."

I smiled and pulled my hand from her head and took a bite from the apple-orange fruit. "Sounds like a plan." Leaning against the tree, Phoebe and I chatted for a few minutes before my eyes drooped as I drifted off to sleep.

Cyrus's howl shifted the moon and the sun as it slowly peeked out from behind the mountains in the Dome. The light that poked over the horizon caused me to stir. I groaned and brought my hands to my face, only to find a fleece throw covering me. I glanced up at a furrowed brow, and tight-lipped Seth standing beside me, leaning against the tree.

"Oh shit," I groaned and facepalmed.

"Yeah, Iris, 'oh shit' is right," he grumbled.

I sighed loudly and pushed myself to stand up, only for Seth to gently pull me to my feet. I shifted my gaze from the ground to his face. A sense of relief washed across me; Seth was not as mad as I had imagined he would be. I smiled at him as trickles of water streamed down his face and dropped from his hair. A hint of a woodsy-scented cologne caught my attention.

"Are you upset with me?" I winced.

Seth ran a hand through his wet hair and shook his head. "Not necessarily, no. You didn't leave the Dome... But the simple fact that you walked out of my line of sight to where any of these creatures could have done something to you..."

"It's okay, I had Phoebe here to keep me company." I dusted my dress off as I pulled my hand from his.

"You mean the griffin that was here?" he asked.

"Mhm. Anyway, how exactly did you find me?"

Seth jutted his chin towards the pack of wolves standing guard at the bottom of the hill. "Lupin told me you two hung out for a bit with the fireflies."

"Oh, but they were so beautiful, though! Can you really blame me?" I flashed a coquettish grin up at him.

"Mhm. Sure, if you say so." Seth took my hand, and we headed towards another area of the Dome. The entire walk, I could see he was visibly restraining himself.

I stopped and pulled my hand from his. "Is this difficult for you, Seth?" I questioned.

He turned around to face me. "It's a lot harder than you think."

I had a sudden urge to hug him. I stepped up to him and jumped, wrapping my arms around his neck and my legs around his waist. I squealed as his hands grabbed my ass, and he fell onto his backside with a big "oof."

I could feel his anger rising, only to come back down to a slight panic once he realized his crotch was perfectly aligned with mine. All that was between us were two pieces of fabric. A seductive smirk crossed his lips, and I scrambled out of his lap.

"You did that on purpose!" I shouted, pushing myself up from the ground.

"Except you're the one who jumped on me!" he playfully shouted back.

A single drop of water fell from the tips of his damp hair. I lifted my finger and willed it to stop before it hit the ground. I brought it to my hand without thinking and stared at it as it glistened in the sunlight.

Seth rose from the ground and dusted himself off while I concentrated on this beautiful, single droplet of life. I brought my hand closer to my face and gazed at it with wide, wondering eyes. "It's… so pretty," I gasped.

My gaze shifted from the droplet hovering above my hand to Seth's surprised face. After losing focus, I released it. "What? Did I do something wrong again?"

Seth blinked, and his brow knitted as his face contorted in a tangle of emotions, like he was trying to gain a sense of what the hell he'd just seen.

"Don't do it." I pointed at him.

"How's your energy?" he simply asked.

I thought for a moment. I didn't feel tired or even exhausted, like I had a few hours ago. "I ate one of those fruits from the bowl you left me, and I feel better than ever!" I twirled around, giggling.

"Combined with a short nap, it'll do that to you. Come on, we have somewhere we need to be." He turned toward the forgotten city and started walking.

I followed him. "Where are we going? Please don't tell me we are going outside of the Dome."

"I have an accidental death to cause, and don't worry. You're not going over to the other side," he said, shoving his hands into his pockets.

I cocked my head as I matched his pace, trying to remember yesterday's events. Then it clicked: the Overlord. "Wait, what are you going to do to him?"

Seth stopped dead in his tracks and craned his neck at me. His head was suddenly that of a jackal, and his body shifted. Large claws grew from his nails. His knees inverted as if he were a dog standing on its hind legs, and an ornate golden headcloth with two pieces of turquoise plated sashes that rested upon his shoulders. "You will know soon enough, my dear." His ethereal voice vibrated the trees and sent ripples through nearby ponds.

I froze in place. My lips parted, and my eyes stared at Seth with great adoration. He now stood roughly as tall as a two-story house, maybe even taller, in his proper form. "And so my guardian reveals his true self to me." I couldn't help but smile.

Chapter 11: Accidental Death

Seth

I stood staring down at Iris. The expression on her face was more adorable than anything I'd seen thus far. I knelt in front of her and offered my palm.

"It'll be much faster than walking and more comfortable than trying to keep up with me," I said, urging her onto my hand.

Iris looked down at my hand then back up at me. "I'd love to!" she squealed and climbed into my hand.

I gently placed her on my shoulder. "Hang on. I don't want to risk you falling off." I smirked before continuing towards the edge of the dome.

"So this," Iris pointed to me. "is this all you?" she asked.

"Yes," I replied. "Is there something wrong with how I look?"

Iris shook her head. "I actually don't mind your true form. Why did you hide it?"
I raised a brow. "Imagine you were back in that glass room. Now picture me stomping down the hallway. You definitely would've had a heart attack." I chuckled.
"That makes sense." She crossed her legs as she sat on my shoulder, all while holding onto my fur.

We continued in silence. The chirps and chitters of small birds nearby were accompanied by the pitter-patter of wolves as they rushed to catch up to us.

looked down, only to see Cyrus and her pack struggling to keep up. "Seth, where are you going?" she huffed.

"To take care of business. What do you need?" I asked, annoyed.

"When you're done, we need to talk… It's about Osiris," she shouted as she steered the pack in the opposite direction.

Osiris? What did he do now? I thought as I felt a tap on the back of my ear. Assuming Iris needed my attention, I shifted my ear in her direction. "Mm?"

"Are we almost there?" she asked innocently.

I looked straight ahead at the border edge and spotted Ra's headdress reflecting the sun. "Yes, we are here." I brought my hand up to my shoulder and urged Iris to step back into my palm. "Come, I'll let you down so I can do what needs to be done."

Her tiny figure climbed into my hand. Kneeling, I let her slide off my fingers and onto a soft spot in the grass.

"Do you trust me?" I asked as she brushed her dress off.

Her head instantly tilted up to face me. "I do… but what do you need me to do?"

"Stay here, and whatever you do, do not come running. I would hate to put you back in danger," I replied. Rising, I walked over to Ra, who was accompanied by Osiris and the Overlord. He looked worse for wear.

Osiris crossed his arms over his chest. His sleep deprived eyes narrowed. "You're late," he grumbled.

I glanced down at him and flashed my canines. "I had my reasons. But we need to make this quick. Little one isn't so patient, and I would hate for her to see this."

"Fuck you, Seth, she will see you for the monster you truly are!" the Overlord shouted, earning him a punch to the gut from Osiris.

"Oh, you boys had better hurry this up. I have some things to do in your temple, Seth," Ra complained. His tired eyes shifted between Osiris and me.

"I'll meet you there, Ra. Just go." I dismissed him with an annoyed tone. My gaze was locked on the Overlord.

"You won't kill me," he coughed.

"You're right, I won't. But they will." I pointed to the soulless on the other side of the Dome. I kneeled and pressed my palm to the dirt to open a portal to the underworld. I smirked, watching the Overlord's face contorting in horror as the undead soldiers that Anubis let me borrow crawled out of the portal.

Some were missing their jaws, others, bits of flesh. Only a few made it to the surface before I closed the portal. They looked to me, awaiting their orders.

"Send him to the other side." I jutted my chin at the Overlord. I watched in satisfaction as they grabbed him by his limbs and head.

The Overlord fought against them, but it was a losing battle. The sudden shuffling of the grass caused everyone to freeze. My soldiers growled and snarled at the intruder. I turned to see that the said intruder was none other than Iris, who I'd told to stay behind. *Damn her curiosity. I knew it would get the best of her.*

"Iris, what are you doing?" I shouted, my anger rising.

Her eyes widened at the sight of the undead. "S-something called me over here..." she stuttered. "Honestly I—I was pulled by something just a moment ago."

My soldiers dropped the Overlord and charged her. Before I could stop them, they had surrounded her... and knelt with their heads bowed. My jaw dropped to the floor.

This, I had not foreseen. I genuinely had feared for her life. Only she seemed calmer than I was. I shifted back to my human form and approached them. They cowered at my feet, as if to apologize. I commanded them to finish what they were ordered to do before taking Iris's hand.

"Don't you ever scare me like that again! I don't know what they would have done if—"

"Seth, I think they know who I am. Since every being here knows of this prophecy, then somehow they do, too," she said, still the picture of a calm I wished I felt. A green orb of light glowed on her forehead, causing me to cock my head in confusion.

I watched my reflection through her eyes. A small object cut through the air, heading directly for me. Iris raised her hand and a wall of stone formed from the ground, to create a blockade between the object and me.

I couldn't believe my eyes. I turned around to see the wall and stepped out from behind it to find a dagger embedded in the stone.

"Earth." Iris smiled, then her eyes rolled to the back of her head, and she collapsed to the ground.

I scooped her into my arms and turned to face the Overlord. He was quickly restrained by my underworldly soldiers. "I have no other words for you," I snarled at him then turned my attention to the soldiers. "Get rid of him."

"Seth, you'll pay for this! You'll all pay for this!" the Overlord shouted as he fought for his life

Each of them grabbed the Overlord and marched through the barrier. They threw him as far into the brush as they could before dropping into their own portals back to the underworld.

A horde nearby quickly approached and grabbed the Overlord. A smirk crossed my lips as I cradled Iris.

I watched in satisfaction while they ripped him apart, limb by limb. The Dome did not transfer sound from the other side, so his screams for help fell on deaf ears. I glanced down at Iris, whose closed eyes spilled tears for a man who deserved nothing more than death itself.

I leaned into her ear, whispering, "Don't worry, that will never happen to you. As long as I am here, I swear, I will protect you with my life."

Iris wiggled and squirmed in my arms. "Put me down. Ra! You owe me answers!" she shouted weakly.

"What's wrong? What answers?" I asked, gently setting her feet on the ground.

"Everything. I need answers for everything, Seth. I'm going insane not knowing what I am, and I know he can least tell me that much," she panted.

"Iris, what is it you need?" Ra said from behind us, causing me to turn around all while guiding Iris.

Her hand squeezed mine as she addressed him. "What the hell was it that the Overlord called me? Elemental? Is that why I can wield three of the four elements? So far it's water, wind, and Earth. Don't tell me there's fire coming soon."

I shifted my gaze from Iris to Ra back to Iris as we awaited his answer. "Iris, why would that be such a big deal?"

Her eyes widened as she slowly craned her neck up at me. "I don't know who I am or what I can do. Figuring all of this out at the last minute is going to cost me more than just energy. If I faint, fall over or I'm caught off guard for a minute you're going to get mad because I wasn't paying attention, or even worse I could die," she spat.

I sighed and gave her a reassuring squeeze. "Okay, I get it. Because you're right, and I would get pissed off if something did happen."

Ra cleared his throat, causing us to look up at him. "Well, I mean it's kind of obvious, Iris. You're a bright woman; I thought you would have figured it out. It seems that the Overlord's magic didn't affect you for very long since your abilities are activating more quickly than we anticipated."

Iris gasped beside me. "So, what exactly are you saying? That all he did was push me enough to awaken faster or something?"

I chuckled at the thought of Iris being stronger than most of the beings on Earth with the elements that make up all that we are. "So you're saying she's strong, but how strong are we talking?"

"You'd be surprised, Seth. She still has one more element to awaken, and it's a feisty one." Ra chuckled before disappearing in a beam of light.

Iris let out a weakened groan. "How much longer is it going to be for my fire to awaken?"

"What are you talking about? You're just about there," I teased.

Iris pouted her lip at me and turned away slowly. "Everything hurts. This pain— every time it courses through me, my body just— " She gripped the sides of her head and shook.

"Why don't you guys just complete your soul tie? It's tough watching her go through this." Osiris's snarky remark caused me to spin around.

"You are one to speak. You're only in it to please yourself. But not today, nor ever, will you take her away from me," I sneered.

Chapter 12: Energy Fades

Iris

I weakly held onto Seth with my back facing the two as they argued. My mind began to wander. Why couldn't I follow a simple order to sit and stay? Sure, I wasn't his dog, but there was the possibility of danger if I disobeyed Seth, especially if he was in his true form. I might be powerful, but so was he.

We were still in utter shock from my magic wall trick. I blinked for a moment as the world stopped spinning and tilting before I tugged on Seth's arm. "Hey, did you see where the wall went?" I asked, trying to switch the subject.

From the corner of my eye, I watched Osiris.

"Oh man, that was surely a magic trick." Osiris clapped his hands once as he closed the distance. His lust-filled gaze fixated on me, sending a chill down my spine.

Seth moved me behind him again. "Yeah, it was pretty great, but we need to go," he commanded with a sneer.

Seth, what's wrong? I don't like when you use that tone.

I don't trust him.

This is your brother we are talking about here.

Yeah, and he was the one who slept with my—

93

He did what?

We will talk about this later.

A frightening sense of possessiveness emanated from Seth as he narrowed his eyes at his brother. It definitely gave me the heebie-jeebies. I narrowed my eyes at Osiris and I turned to leave. *Let's go. I don't want to be here right now. Something doesn't feel right.*

Seth muttered something to Osiris under his breath and quickly followed. "Iris. Your wall, it came from the ground, right?" he asked.

I thought for a moment before answering. "Yeah, but where did it go? Did it just go back into the ground or disappear?" A sharp pain shot across the back of my neck. I winced and brought my hand up to rub the sore spot.

"Iris?" Seth placed his hand on the small of my back. "Are you alright?"

I groaned and rolled my neck for a moment. A wave of nausea washed over me, causing me to stumble. "I don't think I am. I think I used too much energy just then," I slurred.

Seth sighed loudly before picking me up and throwing me over his shoulder nonchalantly. "Well, we have one more stop before we can get back to the house, so bear with me." With that, we dropped into a portal and reappeared in a dimly lit area.

"Where are we?" I asked, cradling my head.

"The temple. The humans know it as King Tutankhamun's tomb," he replied.

Wait, what? Did he just say...? King Tutankhamun? "Wait, wait, wait. No! You can't be serious!"

"Why can't I be serious?" he chuckled, setting me down on a stone block beside the entrance. "How are they unaffected?"

I scanned the area before me. Crowds of people— ordinary, normal people— stood gawking my way.

"Seth, is this the woman Asherah told you about?" A man pointed right at me.

"It is, and she's quite feisty." He winked at me, causing me to blush.

"Come, we have much to discuss, Seth. Your portals aren't holding up as well as we had hoped and one of the books has gone missing." The man shifted his gaze to me, then back to Seth. "I trust that Ra will take care of us until this mission is over."

Seth nodded and walked over to an altar placed in the opposite corner of the temple.

I turned to examine the rest of the area. Sliding down the block, I slowly moved from one corner to the other. I still held my head with one hand. "I never thought I'd live to see this," I whispered.

My curiosity got the best of me as I approached what looked like the opening of a dark pit.

"Iris, watch where you're walking," Seth said, not bothering to look up from what looked to be a gold-plated book.
"Huh?" I turned too quickly and tripped over my own feet. My feet searched for purchase, but found none, and I tipped backward toward the portal, my arms flying out to the sides and grabbing nothing but air.
An arm wrapped around my waist, and Seth yanked me away from the portal. The force of his pull sent me slamming into the wall.

I shouted in pain as the corner of the concrete blocks scraped across my arm. Fear and panic and adrenaline pounded through my veins as I glanced up at Seth and slapped my hand over the wound. I couldn't help but yelp as blood oozed from between my fingers and down my arm.

Seth growled in frustration and turned to the man he'd been speaking to before. "We will continue this later," he grumbled. The man bowed his head and backed away as Seth grabbed me by my waist and jumped into another portal.

We appeared in the middle of the living room of Seth's home. I winced as he simply tossed me onto the couch.

"What's your problem, Seth?" I whined, sitting up. I kept my hand on my wound and squeezed my eyes shut in pain.

"You want to know what my problem is, Iris? You don't fucking listen! You're stubborn to a fault, and you refuse to do something as simple as *stay put!*" he shouted, hands buried in his hair. "You've done nothing but cause trouble since you got here. I can't protect you if you're constantly getting in the way!"

I shifted my gaze to the floor and lowered my head. Tears brimmed my eyes. "I'm sorry," I whispered.

He turned away from me and rushed into the bathroom. The rushing of water sounded for a moment. Seth reappeared with a low growl and stomped over to me. Seth pulled my arm free of my grasp, I yelped at the unexpected touch. He knelt beside me and examined the open wound, then scoffed and raised the wet washcloth he'd brought out with him and cleaned up the spilled blood before wrapping my arm in a bandage.

"Don't leave this building. Cyrus will be posted outside with her pack to keep watch. If Osiris shows up, you need to tell me." With that, he disappeared again.

After Seth jumped into the portal, tears finally spilled from my eyes. I refused to let him hear me cry. I rose from the couch, slipping off my shoes. I walked into my room to change, tears spilling from my eyes and sobs escaping my lips.

I looked around the room after slipping into a silk nightgown I found hanging in the wardrobe and stopped at the foot of the bed. The center of the sheets was still covered in the red elixir. I weakly grabbed the sheet, ripped it from the bed, and threw it into the corner.

Grabbing a blanket from the closet, I plopped onto the bed and curled into a ball under it. A crippling pain coursed through the wound on my arm and over my body like the Nile flooding its banks. I shouted as images of ancient Egypt flashed through my mind. All the gods were gathered around in a circle, but I could not see between them. As the images faded, I slowly drifted off to sleep, wondering for a moment what the message could be.

Hours later, the howl of the wolves caused me to stir. "Mm, it's nighttime already? Is Seth not back yet?" I moaned sleepily, sitting up in bed. I rubbed my eyes, released a quick yawn, and scooted over to the edge of the bed, then swung my feet over.

Are you still at the temple? I asked.

Yes. I'm busy, I'll be back in a bit.

You've been gone since this afternoon. How much longer are you going to be?

I will be back when I'm done. Cyrus is just outside if you want company.

But—

Iris.

I sighed. *Fine.*

I shuffled from around the bed towards the door only to run into something which caused me to stumble and fall backward. A hand wrapped around my waist, catching me before I could fall.

My eyes shot open, and to my surprise, a pair of forest-green orbs stared back at me. "Osiris." I gasped in shock. "What are you doing here? Didn't Seth tell you—"

Osiris clasped his hand around my mouth and signaled for me to hush. "Don't spoil the fun, Iris." He pushed me back toward the opposing wall as his grip on my waist tightened.

I clenched my hand in a weak fist and focused on his blood. I needed him to be incapacitated long enough for me to call out to Seth.

Where are you? Panic laced my transmission.

I'm still in the temple.

Help me, please.

What's wrong?

He's here. Please, Seth, I know you're still upset with me, but please.

Osiris cocked his head to the side and clicked his tongue at me. "You called him, didn't you?" He leaned in so his face mere inches from mine.

I stared at him in terror as my body shook. I pushed him away as best I could, but to no avail. He did not give way, and I had very little energy to fight back.

"You're damn right she did," Seth's voice said as he yanked Osiris away from me and through the wall beside the front door.

I fell to the floor with a squeak. "Why am I literally a target for everyone here? I don't get it! If I'm to save this fucking world, everyone needs to leave me alone!" I cried.

"It's because of that thing we haven't taken care of. He wants you for himself, just like he did... with—" Seth paused.

"Just get him out of here, please. I've had enough life-threatening incidents for one day." I pushed myself up from the floor.

"You must want me to rip you to shreds again, Seth. Honestly, I wouldn't mind it." Osiris appeared in the rubble, dusting himself off.

Seth growled. "Let me remind you, it was I who ripped *you* to shreds. And even if you had gotten your hands on her, you don't quite have the tools to finish the good work, do you?" A cruel sneer crossed his lips. "Or did Isis finally find you a suitable replacement?"

I looked at Seth with a bewildered look, genuinely confused.

"Ha, I'm more of a man than you are! I would have taken it the first night she was in my arms!" Osiris's smirk drove a sliver of rage into my system.

"Fuck you, Osiris!" I shouted, my voice's echo surprisingly weak. "I don't know what your deal is with me or him, but you need to leave us alone." I raised a shaking hand in his direction.

He looked down his nose at me. "Oh really? You know you can't overpower me. I'm a god, remember?"

I focused on what little energy I had left and summoned the power of the wind. I pushed him as far away from the building as possible with a single, mighty gust. "I don't care what you are! You're annoying and unwelcome!" I shouted as my knees buckled.

I managed to catch myself with one arm, panting heavily. The last of my energy drained, I couldn't lift a finger to defend myself against any more attacks. Seth's hulking form filled my vision, anger painted on his face. "I swear, I will kill him the next time I see him."

The agony in my core ignited once again, and I lowered my head to the floor and screamed as I clutched my stomach. "Make it stop! Make this pain stop, Seth, please! I can't take this anymore." A wail tore itself from me.

"Are you sure about what you're asking me to do?" Seth stepped up to me, gently lifting me into his arms.

I nodded. "Do it. I'm tired of this pain; I just want it to go away," I cried.

Seth dropped into another portal, and the two of us reappeared in an unfamiliar place. I stared in wonder at him. He carried me into a room and lay me on the oversized bed. I could not take my eyes off his body admiring the way his muscles flexed with every move he made. Seth stripped first the remnants of his shirt. My desire for him grew in time with the waves of pain washing over me, white-hot agony lancing through me as I gripped the sheets and screamed.

Once I caught my breath, I gazed at him with wide eyes and a trembling lip as he crawled onto the bed, and positioned himself over me. I huffed and panted with a need that only he could satisfy as his hands slipped under the gown, and with one tug, he tore the fabric away, exposing my yearning flesh to him.

Seth took a deep breath, inhaling the scent of my arousal before he wrapped my legs around himself and pulled me up to straddle him. "I'm going to ask you one more time. Is this what you want?"

I nodded and brought my lips to his while he positioned himself at my entrance. I whimpered against his lips as he slowly thrust his hips, my wet folds spreading to welcome his throbbing erection.

My body shook with pain and pleasure. I tilted my head back and released a series of moans and cries of joy. I squealed as the pressure built up between us.

"You're so fucking tight," he grunted and moaned while he leaned forward with one hand supporting my neck. He kissed a trail from my throat to my lips. "You're going to want to hold on. This is going to hurt. Scratch my back, scream if you must, but do not move," he commanded in a husky tone.

I whimpered against his lips and wrapped my arms around his neck as I prepared to give myself to the man chosen to give me his all.

With a buck of his hips, his girthy cock delved deep, I felt a radiating pain within me. I attempted to wiggle and grind against him, only to be held firmly in place while the pain coursed through my hips and back, causing me to pull my lips from Seth's and bite down on the side of his neck. I let out a cry. I dug my nails into the flesh on his back. This virgin body was no match against his larger size.

I shifted my legs as I tried to pull away, and Seth replied with a throaty moan, commanding me to sit as still as possible.

That's it. Let it all out.

It hurts! It hurts so much, Seth, please. I begged, clawing at his back.

Give it a second, shh. He grabbed the base of my neck and held my body close.

I gasped and writhed in his arms as he held me tightly. A light moan escaped my lips with every ragged breath I took.

You... You are mine. Your soul and body belong to me now.

Seth's hips slowly thrust. I could feel every thick inch as he massaged my insides with perfectly timed strokes. My breath quickened, and a knot formed in my core as he picked up his pace, causing me to bounce in his lap.

My arms loosened from around his neck and fell slack against his chest as he gently lowered me to the bed. He brought his hands down to my sides, and with his thumbs pressed against my hips, he held me still.

"Iris, I'm going to fill you with every drop I've got," he said in a low husky tone.

With those simple words, the knot inside of me burst. "Oh my God, Seth!" I screamed as a wave of intense pleasure washed over me. My body clenched around him in severe spasms. His member twitched, flexed, and pumped his seed into me. I arched my back as my muscles spasmed. Seth captured my lips, and we both rode the waves of my orgasm and his release.

He pulled away from me. His lustful gaze stared into my very being.

As he propped himself up on his elbows, he pressed his forehead against mine, our heavy breaths in sync. We gazed into each other's eyes for a moment before he began to pull out.

I let out a soft moan and stopped him before he could. "Please don't move. Just stay here for a moment," I panted. Closing my eyes, I took a moment to calm my erratic nerves.

Seth's lips kissed all over my neck and cheeks and eventually back to my lips. "How's your pain?" he asked in a low tone.

"The fire inside died down. The um..." The heat in my cheeks rose as I thought about the ache that had yet to vanish. "There's this weird ache but it's bearable, for now." I place my hand on my lower abdomen and feel a weird lump. My eyes shot open, and I look down at the source. "Seth... What the hell is that?"

He thrust his hips, and I watched as his girthy length shifted with it. "That's you?" I squeaked. "How is that even possible?" My gaze volleyed between his eyes and his member buried inside me.

"Your body does wonderful things. It seems you're the perfect fit." Seth chuckled when he slowly pulled himself from me, earning him a sing-song of moans.

"Oh!" I exclaimed and shuddered as Seth plopped down beside me and wrapped his arms around me. When he pressed his lips to my forehead, I purred with delight and rolled onto my side, burying my face into his chest.

"You up for another one?" Seth asked.

"What?" I weakly exclaimed. "Another what? How can you have so much energy?" I asked lazily.

Seth chuckled. "It was a joke. Get some rest. We have work to do in the morning." Rolling onto his back, he laid his head back on the pillow and let out a huff.

"I just want to sleep forever," I groaned. "By the way... Where the hell are we?"

Seth reached over and ran his fingers across my abdomen, causing me to giggle. "On the far side of the Dome. Closest to the healing lake. It was supposed to be a surprise, but Osiris ruined it. I couldn't keep you in that building since it's compromised. I will have someone bring our things here while we are out tomorrow.

I threw my leg over his and rested my head on his chest. Smiling, I nodded before drifting off to sleep.

Chapter 13: First Wave

Seth

It happened. It finally happened. Iris had given me her everything. Not just her body, but her soul. She was now mine for eternity.

Her soft snores fanned against my chest as we laid there tangled in one another. I couldn't help but smile when she clung to me harder with every move I made.

I maneuvered the blanket over us and drifted off to sleep.

Sometime later, the howls of Cyrus and her pack indicated that morning had come back around to greet us. I didn't stir until I felt a cold empty spot beside me and opened my eyes to see that Iris was no longer in bed.

I shot up, threw on a pair of pajama pants, and ran out of the room searching for her. Panic filled my veins until I heard a stream of water cut off from the bathroom. I stopped and waited for her to emerge.

"Iris, are you okay in there?" I called out to her.

"I'm okay, just a little sore," she replied as she opened the door, clutching a towel she'd wrapped around herself. "Am I supposed to feel like I got hit by a freight train?"

I let out a breath I hadn't realized I was holding and approached her. "Not necessarily, but since it was your first time screwing a god, things are going to be a little off for you. Besides, I think we unbound your abilities.

"I hope I don't feel like this for too long. I really need to figure out this whole saving the world thing," she groaned.

"Well, that's what we're going to do today. Are you okay with doing some energy work? I want to test the limits of your abilities. If not, we can work on something else."

She shrugged. "We can try, but we probably won't get too far." She winced with each step as she made her way to the room.

A knock came from the front door. "Stay right there, Iris. Give me a second, and I'll help you.

I ran down the stairs and over to the door. I opened it to none other than Ra, a grin painted on his face.

"I don't need the lecture, Ra. What do you need?" I raised my brow at him.

"Oh, no, I don't need anything. What I want you to do today is keep a low profile. Osiris is on the verge of losing his mind after last night's stunt," he growled.

"Well, he can't have something he has no soul-tie to. So bring it on, I've been itching for a proper fight." I smirked.

"Oh trust me, he knows, and so does the entire Dome." Ra laughed as he playfully nudged me. "Seth, I just want you to know, anything is possible. Even love." He smiled as he turned to take his leave.

"Sometimes I wish I wasn't out here guarding your house, Seth." Cyrus rolled her eyes at me as she rose from the porch and stretched. "Ya freaking sickos. I also took the liberty of bringing all of your things over once you two fell asleep."

"Hey, Cyrus? You have your mate, so why am I getting shit for something you do daily? You fucking hypocrite!" I shook my head and shut the door, only to open it again for a moment. "Thanks for that."

Closing the door, I quickly made my way over to Iris, whose legs were shaking as she leaned against the door frame, and snaked my hand around her waist. "C'mon, let's get you dressed and find something to eat. Those fruits should have almost eliminated your hunger by now."

Iris placed her hand on mine as she took careful steps towards the edge of the bed. She slowly turned around and sat down, letting out a heavy breath. "Oh goodness, this is a pain."

I released my hold on Iris, ran into the kitchen, grabbed a purple fruit and a glass of the healing elixir, then ran back into the room. "Here, this should help, and that fruit tastes like grapes, so eat up." I handed her both items and turned around to sift through the closet. "Why did she make all of these fucking dresses?" I grumbled.

"I don't mind wearing dresses... Let's go with the gray one today." She pointed it out to me.

"Nope, you're glowing today, so we shall go with..." I scanned over the stupid colors and finally found one that suited her energy. "...this one." I pulled a burgundy floor-length dress and the matching sandals and laid them on the bed next to her.

"How in the world are you so nifty with these sorts of things?" she giggled.

"I'm not a complete asshole, Iris. I like to help when I can," I replied with a shrug.

"So what did the Overlord mean when he said I'd see the monster in you eventually?" she asked.

I froze and turned to face her. "Well, I don't think he meant anything specifically." My treacherous hand rubbed the back of my neck.

Iris huffed and rose. "Seth, after last night, do you really think you can lie to me about something as serious as this?" She dropped her towel and leaned over to grab the dress.

I cocked my head at her and narrowed my eyes as I stared at her back in confusion. "Iris, don't move!" I commanded, and I knelt behind her. The formation of a pyramid connected across her lower back from the two diamond-shaped birthmarks on her hips. "What the hell is this?" I muttered.

"What's wrong? Is there something on my back?" She peeked over her shoulder at me.

I sighed and pressed my lips to the center of the pyramid and trailed all the way up her back to her neck, earning me a mixture of light gasps and moans. "We will have to ask Asherah about this later." I comforted her before grabbing the dress from her hands. "Here, let me help."

She slumped her shoulders in defeat. "I hope that fruit kicks in soon. Also, what is that red stuff you keep giving me?"

"It's an elixir to help rebuild your strength and clear your mind," I explained as I slipped the dress over her head.

"Ah." She nodded before slowly turning to face me. "How do I look?"

"I suggest you put your hair up today." I smirked as I turned to leave the room. After last night, I definitely needed to shower, and the sheets definitely needed to be switched out.

"Wait, why should I put my hair up?" Iris asked innocently.

Giving her a quick glance, I shrugged. "Maybe because I like it better when it's up." I went straight into the bathroom and turned the water on before I pulled my pajama pants off and tossed them to the side, only to step in a puddle of water. "Why is everything in here wet?" I grumbled.

"Sorry!" Iris's voice was muffled from the other side of the door.

The water droplets from the floor, wall, and mirror rose from their places and deposited themselves into the sink, leaving every other surface besides the actual shower dry.

I threw the bathroom door open and poked my head out. "Iris, did you just...?" I pointed to the bathroom.

Iris paused her hand mid-braid. "Yes. Why?" She blinked at me innocently.

"Nope, never mind." I pulled away from the door and closed it behind me. "Water, I keep forgetting." I place my head into the palm of my hand. Washing up quickly, I turned off the water, grabbed a towel from the shelf, and dried off before wrapping it around my waist and exiting the bathroom, only to find Iris on the couch, fast asleep.

"Well there goes that idea out the window," I mumbled as I made my way to my room to get dressed.

"I'm awake," she mumbled, blinking and rubbing her eyes. "Just waiting for you to finish up. Did you really expect me to stand and wait for you when my legs are noodles?"

I laughed to myself as I pulled a black T-shirt over my head. "I didn't even expect you to stay awake this long." I strapped my holsters in place along my torso and legs, then pulled on my jacket and my Kevlar over it. Boots... Those were by the door. I grabbed my helmet before heading toward the foyer to grab my boots.

"You get dressed fa..." Iris' stare fell on me as she scanned me from head to toe. "Why do you use guns when you can just summon the undead?"

I shrugged. "I don't like to waste my energy. I'm already using a lot to keep those portals open to my temples."

She opened her mouth to say something, then waved her hand at me.

"What? You had a question."

Iris sat still for a moment before asking, "What exactly is going on in the temples that you needed to keep portals opened? Like the one I almost fell into?"

I smiled. "No, it's a good question. The simple answer is logistics. When the darkness came and filled the skies, I sent my people into the temples to shield them from everything coming their way. That's why there were quite a few people down there. I had to make sure they were safe and remained unaffected. I did not want to lose what little bit of mankind we have left."

"So, the portals supply them with air circulation and food?"

I nodded. "Sunlight for their gardens, water for hydration, washing, and waste management."

Iris smiled at me and rose from her place on the couch. "Well, they definitely appreciate you and respect you more than you could ever know." She approached me and took my hand. "You are a God people will admire more than the others after all of this is over. We will rebuild, and it will be an even better civilization than before."

My heart swelled with pride, and my eyes watered. I had never imagined this woman would be able to bring me to my knees in happiness, and yet I'd give her my life if she wanted it. I smiled and ran my fingers through her hair, swallowing back the emotion rising within me. "Let's get going.

Iris chuckled and nodded. "Yes, let's."

Chapter 14: Fireplay

Iris

We stood staring at the border of the dome where Seth had sentenced the Overlord to a brutal death. My palms became sweaty as my anxiety gripped my heart.

I didn't want to cross over, but I didn't have much choice in the matter. I needed to manage my energy levels and see how much of this dead city I could wipe out.

"So, what are we doing?"

Seth drew his weapon of choice. Today it was an automatic assault rifle. "I will cover you while you take out this corner of the city. With each section you clear, we extend the Dome, until the Earth is ready for the revival ritual," he said calmly.

I inhaled a deep breath and exhaled as I stepped through the Dome and onto the other side. My eyes scanned the dead brush ahead of us, and I gasped, bringing my hand to my mouth as I spotted the Overlord's decapitated head and shredded limbs. "Oh no," I whispered.

Seth cocked his head at me to gauge my reaction. "Seems like they didn't take the body with them. What a pity."

I closed my eyes. I needed to shut out the image of his widened, fearful eyes and bloodstained neck. Twirling my hand, the ground rumbled as I summoned vines and moss to encase and drag his head and limbs under the surface for their own nourishments. "Might as well put you to use then," I muttered.

My bottom lip quivered. "Seth, let's hurry this up, I don't want to be out here longer than we need to be," I mumbled, taking a step

109

forward. My foot landed on a dead branch, causing it to loudly snap. A soulless man nearby screeched as his figure appeared from the tree line ahead.

I threw my hand up and blasted him back with a forceful wind while Seth took him out with a single headshot. We continued walking over fallen brush and debris. A thick tree stump had broken off about double if not triple Seth's height, in the air.

"Hey, could you toss me up there?" I pointed up to the tree.

Seth glanced up at the tree then back at me, lowering the rifle. "What for?" He put a hand on his hip.

"I'll be out of their range, but you'll still be able to spot them and take them out without hitting me," I explained.

He stopped for a moment. "Okay, come." He wrapped his arm around me and gently tossed me up onto the tree.

Upon landing on the top. I squeaked as I balanced myself on the stump. I took a moment to check the distance between me and the ground. "Oh dear," I spotted a small horde charging for us from the other side of the dead brush and pointed them out to Seth. "Over there, a small group of eight."
Seth spun, his breath steady as he quickly raised his firearm and took aim. His stance held sturdy with every pull of the trigger. It was as if the recoil had no effect on him, and he took them out with ease before lowering the steaming muzzle.

I smiled down at him and turned to the forgotten yet destroyed city. I then tilted my head to the sky, focusing my energy on the wind to clear the black clouds containing the biochemical particles that were spread across the sky. The swirling of leaves and debris picked up and blew towards the center of a hurricane that formed over the city.
Where should I push this chemical crap? Is there a body of water nearby?
Send it farther out. We will take care of it eventually.

No, I want to take care of it now.

Iris, stop.

I growled, focused on the closest body of water, and moved the hurricane over a small lake nearby. I watched as the skies over the city cleared, then I glanced down at Seth for a moment before turning back to the city.

"Iris, don't overexert yourself!" he shouted. Time seemed to slow down as his rifle jolted in his hands, the bullet casings ejected slowly as he continued mowing down more and more of the soulless advancing on our position.

I ignored him and tried to regain focus on a larger body of water on the other side of the city. A tingling sensation rushed into waves from my elbows to my fingertips. I stopped for a moment and looked at my hands. The centers of my palms turned red as what looked like a swirling flame dancing in the center. Smiling to myself, I concentrated on the trees just a few feet from me, raised my arm, and moved it in a circular motion. An inferno erupted in the trees as a familiar sharp pain struck the back of my neck.

I winced as I brought my hand up to rub the sore spot on my neck. "Why does this keep happening? Honestly, this is getting ridiculous," I shouted.

"Iris!" Seth's voice came from below.

My nose began to run as I shifted my attention to Seth. "What? Did I do something else wrong?"

"What the hell? Why is your nose bleeding!"

I raised a brow in confusion but the taste of iron lingered on my lips as I wiped away the fluid. I glanced down at my hand and confirmed my suspicion. "Well that's not a good sign."

My head swirled, my vision blurred, and the images of a raging fire atop a large body of water flashed in the back of my mind. I stumbled backwards and lost my footing, as I had forgotten how narrow the tree was.

"Seth! Oh my god!" My arms flailed as I descended toward the ground.

"Damn it, Iris," he growled when I dropped into his arms. "You gotta stop doing that." He pushed his visor up, staring at me with narrowed eyes.

I pressed my hand to my chest while I leveled my breathing. Shifting my gaze, I watched as the fire I created engulfed the trees ahead. "And it looks like I wield fire, too." I pointed at the blazing inferno that was slowly moving toward the city.

Seth's eyes went wide when the fire formed a protective ring around us. I laid my head back onto the ground and broke out in hysterical laughter. This situation I was dragged into— the war, my abilities, everything—became the laughingstock of my hysteria. I finally broke.

"What's gotten into you?" Seth shouted at me.

I couldn't help but laugh. Holding my ribs as they ached, I wasn't sure what had gotten into me either. "I—I can't stop laughing, Seth!" *This is all too much. Everything is too much. You're too much for me. This responsibility, all of it.*" Too much!" I managed between breaths.

He sighed and helped me to my feet before dropping us into a portal. As we emerged in our home, I still couldn't stop gripping my sides, doubled over in laughter.

"What am I going to do with you?" Seth shouted and set me down on the couch in our living room. "Since we're here, let me take a look at your arm." He reached for it.

The laughing fit finally released me, and I flinched away from his touch. "What the heck was that?" At his serious look, I hiccupped, wiped my eyes, then added, "Don't be upset please."

Seth's chest vibrated with a growl. "I don't know what the hell is so funny, but you need to get a grip before I do something you will not like." He narrowed his eyes at me once more.

I hiccupped again. A giggle escaped, despite my best attempts to tamp it down.

Seth's negative energy pushed the air from my lungs, causing the last few bubbles of laughter to come to an abrupt halt. I struggled for a moment, terror rising, then finally gasped an even breath.

To my relief, I was able to fix him with a glare. *Why would you do that?*

Your laughing was out of control.

And now my breathing is, you jerk!

A muscle twitched in Seth's cheek. *Get over it.*

What the hell is with you today?

I finally regained my composure and steadied my breathing. "You didn't have to do that, you know." I scowled at Seth before lying down on the couch.

"How did you know that fire wasn't going to backtrack toward us?" Seth asked.

I simply rolled over on the couch, turning my back to him. "I had a feeling, okay? What else can I say? Did I know that wall was going to protect you from that dagger? No. Did I know my tears were going to kill that creature? Hell no." I sat up quickly and rose from the couch, my temper boiling. "I don't have any fucking answers about what happened today. I don't have any answers from the last couple of fucking days.

"The last thing I remember, I was sitting on the beach in the sun on with my feet in the sand and a good book in my hand," I explained.

"When the water receded, I didn't even take notice until someone tried to drag me away from it. I held my ground, and all of a sudden, it was like my body knew what to do. I commanded the wave to level, and that's when I got sucked into this... This horrible world with its monsters and demons. With its gods and its..." I waved my hand around, tears of loss joining the tears of sadness on my cheeks. "...It's everything."

Seth approached me and sat on the couch, wrapping his arm around me. "Iris, I'm sorry."

"Seth, you just don't understand. You spent the last twelve years looking for a woman who you think is a constant pain in your ass. You stuck around long enough to get what you wanted from me, and now everything is going to fall apart, and I—I don't know what to do! The man who held me captive, I don't even know if he's dead or if he's still out there searching for me, knowing I slipped from the hands of his lousy guards and biochemists..." I bit my lower lip and turned my eyes to the ceiling as tears brimmed once more. "I can't do this, and you know it." I sniffled.

Seth leaned down and kissed the top of my head. "Look, I didn't know you went through all of that. I wasn't told much about your arrival, let alone your location. Every time I'd get close, you would disappear again. I didn't even think I'd ever find you, yet here you are in the flesh. Protecting you is a pain in the ass because it's like you go looking for trouble, not to mention how it's homed in on your location the moment you step foot outside of this Dome."

I closed my eyes and took a deep breath. "Meanwhile, the shit they did to me when I was in their hands... I felt like a fucking lab rat. The constant prodding and poking for their precious database..." I bolt upright, a memory sparking. "Seth, they had a profile filled with information about me. They had more, files and files, enough to be information about everyone in this Dome!"

"What? How the hell could they have information on everyone here? Unless..." Seth rose from the couch, his fists clenched. "That fucking bastard."

I wiped the tears from my eyes as I shifted my gaze to him. "What? Did you remember something?"

He turned to face me. "Do you remember the first day you were here? When I brought you here, what did the Overlord say?"

I thought for a moment before it hit me. "He had been searching for me." I couldn't believe this at all. Everything that happened until today was planned. "That man is going to find me. If he hasn't already, he knows I'm here!"

Seth knelt in front of me, grasping my hands. "Not if I can help it, Iris. I need you to calm down. No one is going to take you away from me, ever, and that is a promise."

"Seth, he's going to kill me! Nothing from this timeline is not meant to survive. Not even you. I have to leave here. I'm putting you all in danger," I cried. Anxiety, panic, and fear all poured into my mind, body, and soul, causing me to shake uncontrollably. I brought my hands to my head and gripped my hair by the roots as the pressure built. Finally, I released a gut-wrenching scream that shook the surface of the Earth.

I inhaled a shaky breath, only to have my hands pried from my head and my lips coated in familiar warmth. Seth. His lips moved against mine as they danced their dance. I let every single bottled-up emotion pour out of me in the form of my spilled tears and muffled cries. Seth pulled away, breaking our kiss only for my arms to pull him back to me. "Promise me you won't leave. Promise I will not walk the path of the undead you command in the Underworld," I whimpered in his ear.

Seth wrapped his arms around me and squeezed me tightly. "I promise to protect you with my life. You are not going anywhere."

"I hope not," I sniffled.

Chapter 15: According to Plan

Osiris

I rolled my eyes and opened a portal to the temple. I knew I needed the Book of the Dead to solidify my contract with him.

Portú cleared his throat when I appeared beside the altar as I reached for the book.

"And what are you doing here? I thought Seth was going to be performing this... Ritual?" he hissed.

I shrugged my shoulders and asked. "He asked me to bring him the book for something or other. So that's what I'm here to do. Is there a problem with that?"

His dark figure appeared from the shadows and his yellow eyes narrowed at me. "I don't see why he would need it now."

"He asked me to grab it for something else he has going on. Didn't you hear? They brought back a girl from one of the facilities outside of the Dome. So, he asked me to grab it."

Portu's eyes closed for a moment before he receded back into the darkness. "Don't leave with that book, Osiris."

I rolled my eyes, snatched the book off the altar and dropped into a portal back to the main building of the Dome.

Once inside I headed straight for the secure levels upstairs and made sure no one else saw me. Or at least anyone else in this building. "Oh, this is going to be a grand ole time." I snickered to myself.

I counted the numbers on the doors when I had passed by them. I had a thing for odd numbers and settled for room 103. It couldn't be divided by an even number which in turn, made me giddy to finish this task.

Hell, who wouldn't like to scare the living shit out of Iris?

I tossed the obsidian Book of Death onto a wooden table nearby. The heavy book broke through the table and dropped straight onto the tiled floor with a heavy stone clank. I turned and gave the book an unamused look. "I forgot how heavy that fucking thing was." I muttered.

Before I could think of a way to cause Iris to panic an idea popped into my mind. "I could summon Nephthys… Oh this is going to be great!"

I strode over to where the book had fallen and snatched it off the floor and flipped it open to the scripture 'Summoning of the dead' and began scanning over the stone page. "That seems easy enough."

I opened a small window like portal to watch the brutal attack on Iris. "Awe, poor little girl tried to take a nap."

I laughed through the whole ordeal of summoning the soul of Nephthys. Granted, I had conceived a child with her, but she was Seth's beloved. After her passing, I couldn't help but wonder how much more I could put Seth through. I wanted Iris to hate him for something I had done, and I wasn't about to stop now. The only thing I could think of was to bring her soul back to torture the poor woman.

"Oh, this couldn't get any better." I smirked, glancing over at the book of the dead.

Surely, Ian needed it to bring back human souls to bring his clones to life. But something in the back of my mind couldn't figure out why the man looked so goddamned familiar. I scratched my chin in thought as I awaited his arrival in the Beijing facility.

"Look what we have here!" Ian's voice shouted joyfully as he approached.

"Ian." I gave him a nod before turning my gaze back to the machines whirling around the building.

Ian clapped my shoulder as he stood beside me. "Isn't it a beautiful sight to see?" He smirked. "There are multiple facilities around the world with the same clones. My army will be unstoppable."

"So, what exactly is the purpose for this, Ian?" I cocked a brow at him, leaning against the railing. "The only reason I agreed to help you was to make my brother miserable."

Ian released his hand from my shoulder, shoving both fists into his pocket. "Well, you see, Osiris, I am stronger than those abominations in that Dome of theirs. They don't deserve to live. This planet was meant for one race of beings, and that's us humans. You, on the other hand, I can't kill, so I decided to make you an ally."

What the hell? And this is why we left you humans to die. I rolled my eyes and scoffed. "And what is it you need from me?" I asked, straightening my posture.

"Did you bring that book I asked you about?" He pulled one hand from his pocket, to point at the bag beside me.

"I did. But again, what do you need from me?" With every word that left his mouth, my patience wore thinner. I had this gnawing feeling in the back of my mind that Ian himself didn't appear to be human. His thin lips and flattened cheekbones reminded me of a bird. This poor and confused man.

"Take Iris out of Seth's hands and bring her to me. It's simple, really." He chuckled once more.

I narrowed my eyes at him as I watched him from the corner of my peripheral view. "It's been a challenge, actually. They're soul-bound now, and it's getting harder to get her alone." Reaching down for the bag, I cocked my head in his direction as he jumped onto the railing and perched like a bird.

I shook my head in utter confusion at the man. "Ian, are you sure you're human?"

"Last time I checked I was. Why?" He pulled a cigarette out of his shirt pocket and lit it.

I grabbed the bag and threw it at him. "You sure don't act like one," I scoffed and turned to leave. "I'll get you what you want, as long as you keep your end of the deal." I gave him a half-assed wave and I exited the facility.

"I'll keep my end, as long as I get the girl!" he shouted after me.

I thought of our original bargain. Being king of the world was something I looked forward to. The massive statues of Egypt's truly and the riches. Not to mention the choice of women. I just needed my father, Seth, and Iris out of the way.

Ian

Once Osiris had left me to das I saw fit. I wondered why the bastard was so eager to help me get rid of them all. I shrugged off the feeling, knowing damn well I had information on how to kill him too, once the time came around.

How much longer were these bodies needing to grow? I wondered while I shifted my gaze down at the incubators below.

I took a drag from my cigarette. The burning end seared and sizzled and the ember glowed bright.

"I wonder if my other facility is ready," I spoke aloud. A sharp pain shot across the base of my neck, causing me to groan as I rolled my shoulders. An image of a burning structure flashed in the back of my mind, and a man's voice screeched through the darkness.

Ian, where the fuck are you?

Ha, you would love to know, wouldn't you, dear Uncle.

I swear to all of the energy in this fucking universe I will take you back and you will be tried for treason and murder.

You have to find me first.

The memory of my last conversation with my so-called uncle echoed in the back of my mind. Murder? Treason? I'd had an ordinary life before my parents were killed by those bastards. But the crimes that he had accused me of were not a part of that.

"Soon, everything will be restored to its glory. The world will flourish, and everyone will bow down to me as their savior!" I rose, balancing myself on the railing as I lifted my arms to the sky.

Chapter 16: Uncontrollable Fear

Seth

After a few hours of uncontrollable sobs, Iris held onto me as her body wound down from her panic attack. I was finally able to settle her nerves and get her thoughts back in order. She had fallen asleep on top of me, her legs straddling me and her head resting in the crook of my neck. I slowly rose from the couch and walked up the stairs. I figured she could use the rest, so I lay down with her on my chest, leaning back against the headboard.

Iris purred in my ear and gently clawed at my chest. I raised an eyebrow at her. Was she not asleep? I gently ran my fingertips along her backside, causing her to arch and wiggle her hips. Her thighs brushed against my groin as she slid off of my torso and curled into my side.

"Are you awake?" I mumbled, trying to adjust myself as my growing erection sprang into action. She carelessly pulled herself back on top of me and kissed my neck, awakening the beast.

I hiked up her dress and grabbed at her shorts as she nibbled on my neck. I gave her a warning growl, only for her to moan in my ear.

"I need you," she whispered, pulling away from me and gazing at me with darkened, lustful eyes.

I stared back and realized there wasn't a hint she was awake. More so, she was still asleep in her own mind.

Iris licked her lips and pressed her forehead against mine. Her eyes stared into my soul. "Is there something wrong?" Her voice had changed. The sapphire in her eyes swirled, her ethereal tone caused my cock to twitch.

Is her water element present? I thought.

"How would you know anything about that, Seth?" Iris replied, confirming my suspicion.

"I've watched you. Long enough to know that you need something from me." I gripped the sides of her shorts and ripped them apart at the seams.

Iris's water form reached down and unzipped my pants, freeing my throbbing erection and positioning it at the entrance of her soaking wet pussy. I grabbed her thighs and rammed my cock deep inside of her with one go. Iris clawed at my arms, and she threw her head back and moaned.

I thrust into her slowly this time, massaging her insides while her lips captured mine. She purred and released muffled moans when I hit her sweet spot.

My, my, little one, you've missed me, hmm?

Iris nodded a second before she hit her climax. Her vaginal walls held onto me like a vise, causing me to release my seed. My cock flexed inside her as my grip on her hips tightened, holding her in place.

The two of us lay still, panting as Iris faded in and out of consciousness. When I attempted to lift her, Iris's thighs clamped down around my waist, as if she didn't want to move.

Well, that was easy, I thought as I lay my head back against the headboard.

She slept on my chest for hours while. I ran my fingers through her hair, it's softness and strength playing about in my hands. Grabbing a single strand, I twirled it around, causing her to stir.

She let out a sharp breath and groaned as she tried to sit up, but I pulled back down. "Nope, you get to lie here for a little while longer."

Iris whined sleepily and pressed her face to my bare chest. "But I need to stretch. My back is killing me."

I leaned into her ear while my free hand stroked her hip. "That's because I'm buried deep inside of you right now," I said in a husky tone.

Iris propped herself up on her elbows. Strands of her hair fell over her face. "What? When did we...?" She shifted her hips to confirm my words. "Seth, oh!" She lay her head back down on my chest, her cheeks burning with embarrassment, and sat still for a moment.

"You were hysterical. I tried to calm you down, but that didn't work. I tried to let you rest, but your water element came to the surface." I stroked her back as I explained. "You whispered something in my ear and, uh woke the beast." I gave her a teasing thrust, earning myself a wiggle and a moan.

"I'm still trying to figure out how you're so fucking big, Seth," she mumbled under her breath, thinking I couldn't hear.

I chuckled to myself. "You know, in this human form, I'm well over six foot seven inches in height, and a God at that. Were you expecting something much smaller between my legs?" I bucked my hips into her again. "You're what, five foot three inches tall? Of course it's going to be big."

"Oh! Seth, stop moving, please, I'm gonna—" she begged, panting.

Wrapping an arm around her, I flipped us over and leaned in dangerously close to her neck, my lips grazing her ear. "You're going to what? Cum for me again and again?" I seductively growled and began thrusting into her.

Iris squealed and squirmed beneath my frame as my hands gripped her waist, pulling her onto me. She wrapped her arms around my neck to keep me close while she moaned and cried with pleasure into my ear.

I pulled away from her neck, bringing my lips to hers with a sense of urgency, slipping my tongue into her mouth her petite hands clawed at my back.

Her clitoris formed a knot at the base of my shaft and her walls tightened around me. I prepared for a release. I growled with pleasure and slowed the movement of my hips.

The warmth of my heart spread joy throughout my body. The words I wanted to tell her slipped from me: "I love you," I whispered into her lips as I kissed her.

Her pounding heartbeat fluttered in my ears with excitement and joy as those words drew us closer. Those simple words turned her body into overdrive, and she whispered back, "I love you, too."

I froze for a moment and pulled away from her. Were my ears deceiving me? Did she just say it back without hesitation? My hooded eyes stared at her with adoration. "You do?"

Iris nodded, "I do," she replied, smiling at me. "Oh my god!" she exclaimed as I slowly pulled myself from her soaking wet pussy and, with one swift motion, rammed myself back into her with rapid thrusts and a sudden, overwhelming need to use her body to milk every drop of cum from me.

"Yes, Iris, I am your god," I growled huskily as we finished off the day in pure bliss.

--

Months had passed since the day I found her. The woman who Asherah had appointed to me to locate, protect, and even come to love. Even with her flaws, she won my heart over again and again. Losing her would mean I would have to live out the rest of eternity alone. I couldn't bear the thought as we traveled worldwide, starting with the west coast of the United States.

Together, we'd been able to clear the land, extend the Dome, and prepare the Earth for her restoration in Canada, Alaska, and Southern America. We prepared to head east from this state called New York towards Africa, Europe, and eventually Asia. Iris became more confident in using her abilities and learned to manage her energy levels as she burned down old cities, blew away the chemical-ridden clouds that hung overhead, and washed away the debris day after day without fail.

I couldn't have been more proud to be her guardian. Hell, I never would have believed that she would come to love me as much as I had come to love her. Over time, as we cleared these cities, I noticed mythical tattoos appearing more and more over her body. It still puzzled us as to where they were coming from and why. Asherah ignored my calls regarding this question.

"Iris?" I called out to her. My eyes scanned the surrounding area. "Where are you?"

Iris poked her head out from behind a building we were preparing to search. "Yes? I'm right here," she replied.

I chuckled at the single stand of snow-white hair falling over her face from the messy bun she had thrown her hair into before we left that morning. "You know, you're fucking adorable, and that's weird coming from me."

Her cheeks flushed a deeper shade of pink before she stepped out from behind the building and hopped over the dead bodies of the soulless. "Well, it's not like I'm trying to be adorable. This extremely long head of hair is driving me insane."

"Throw it in a braid like you usually do, then. I'll keep an eye out." I leaned down and kissed the top of her head, then reloaded my firearms.

I watched as she turned around in her black combat boots, black quarter-sleeve T-shirt, and matching cargo pants. Pulling her hair free from its confinement, she quickly ran her fingers through it before making a braid. "So, how do you like this look compared to the dresses? I know it's not traditional for a supernatural or an elemental to wear non-customary clothing, but this feels so much better." She turned to face me.

"Well, you look good in everything you wear, from dresses to combat gear, so… don't ask me that again."

Iris stuck her tongue out at me as she adjusted her belt. Her head snapped to the side as a barrage of footsteps and mindless groaning approached. "We have company."

I took aim and began firing off rounds. Blood splattered across the ground and nearby buildings. The soulless dropped like flies as I advanced forward, quickly replacing my magazine. "Get into the building now!" I shouted, but Iris stood frozen in place, staring at something off in the distance.

I turned in the direction she was looking, and my eyes landed on a figure. It was a human man with the fingers of one hand hooked onto his belt and what looked to be a walkie-talkie in the other. His raven-black hair was slicked back, his eyes were bright yellow, and his features reminded me of a bird. Slender cheekbones and pointed nose contributed to the illusion, but his build was slender.

I shouted, "Shit. Iris, we gotta go!" I ran over to her and grabbed her hand before heading off into the building.

"He's finally found me, Seth. What the hell do I do?" she whispered fearfully.

"We kill him and everyone he just called to come after you. Simple," I replied as we carefully moved through the two-story building. The hallways were littered with trash, broken furniture, and the bodies of its previous occupants. The wretched stench caused both Iris and I to pull our facial covers over our noses as we muscled through the foul odor.

After trekking through a labyrinth of hallways we stopped at the corner and stared down to the end of the hallway. I closed my eyes and took a deep breath. The room ahead resembled the one I'd found her in.

126

Broken glass was scattered across the grungy, bloodstained floor, and several bodies lay face down on the inside.

Iris's breath hitched. *No, no, no, not again.* I could hear her panicking thoughts.

"Iris, I know what you're thinking, but we can't stop here. We gotta keep moving," I urged.

I grabbed her by the arm and stalked off toward the room, kicking the remnants of the glass door. It shattered. Releasing my hold on Iris, I approached the computer on the right side of the room. "It's gotta be here somewhere." I searched, flipping books and paperwork everywhere.

"She's alive. This one is still alive, Seth. We have to take her back with us!" Iris exclaimed.

"Huh?" I turned to the hospital bed, and there was a teenage girl lying unconscious with a tube from her arm attached to a machine and electrodes pasted to her head. "Shit." I finally found what we'd come here for: a tablet that held all the information that the Overlord had handed over to these bastards. I also snatched the external hard drives beside the monitors and stuffed them into my cargo pockets.

I grabbed the girl without disconnecting anything from her body, only to freeze as the clicking of heeled shoes came from the end of the hallway. Iris and I spun to face the man responsible.

"Oh my dear, you're leaving so soon?" he called out.

Why does his voice sound familiar? My eyes narrowed as I scanned this man head to toe. "You're fucking kidding me. The Overlord had a twin?"

"He was more of a clone, per se. I am the original." An evil smile painted across his face as his gaze shifted to Iris. "Aren't you going to come and welcome me? You and I did spend quite a bit of time together."

"You held me captive for twelve years, and you expect me to greet you? Are you insane?" she shouted, anger masking her terror.

"On the contrary, I am. You see, without you in this world, I would have been able to kill all of these disgusting monsters and I can release my clones so they can ride out this one world order to purge the tainted." He smirked. "People like you." He pointed.

"Why would you even bother, if all of the humans are dead? You didn't have to murder the innocent!" I sneered.

The man clasped his hands together and stepped forward. "You see, we did all of this research on every Starseed there is. I have a weakness listed for every single one of them, which makes their extermination much easier. You are all abominations. With my cloning technology, I can ensure the population will be as pure as they come. See, humans have the capability to be stronger than you filthy creatures."

"Artificially grown clones... They live, breathe, make love, work, and everything in between without fighting back until the day they die," Iris whispered. "You sick son of a bitch. What did you do to me?"

The man laughed. "Nothing, yet. I wasn't able to synthesize your abilities due to the simple fact that you kept destroying everything. But when you killed the last guard who was supposed to keep an eye on you until my return, you showed me that you were different from the rest. So, I captured and killed as many of the survivors as I could. Your power would have been able to wipe out the existence of these creatures, and I would have killed you right after."

"Then why would you keep her for twelve years? You knew she wasn't going to be able to stay sedated, let alone sleep the entire time," I growled.

"Seth, every time I got close enough to unlock her abilities, you showed up and she would wake up and make those cute noises she makes with you now. So, I had to keep moving her. The whole reason I sent a modified clone after you was to lock whatever abilities you had and bring you back to me."

I scoffed at his remark. *What Iris does with me, she does with no other man.* "You think you know her so well?"

The man placed a hand on his chest, giving me a look as if I had offended him. "Oh, Seth, is that a hint of jealousy I hear?"

Before I could answer, Iris started in on him.

"Y-you wanted to k-keep me to help you k-kill the remaining Starseeds? Is t-that what y-you're saying?" Iris stuttered. "It makes no sense. You're a lunatic. A power-hungry lunatic. You humans are fucking weak!"

"Well, I knew the gods would intervene. After all, Seth, it was your wife who guided my son's soul to the underworld. She died because you let her out of your sight, and she was not meant to be down there to begin with. But if I can purge the world of this disease that you call supernatural, then so be it."

My anger poured into my veins. I had not known that it was his soul that caused Nephthys to perish. I wanted to kill this son of a bitch slowly and painfully. Iris gazed up at me with fearful eyes.

"You will never lay another finger on her because she's never leaving my side," I threatened as I grabbed Iris and the girl and dropped into a portal back to the Dome.

Ra, I need you to come to get this girl.

Who is it?

I won't know until I find her file.

So, you grabbed the information?

Well, it was on a tablet and a hard drive. I'm sure you'll figure it out. Now move it. I have something to take care of.

I'll see if I can get any information off of the tech while you're gone. Good luck.

129

Chapter 17: Cleansing

Iris

When Asherah explained what these symbols on my back, a deep, familiar feeling was kindled inside me.

In the other timeline, I'd had moments when things didn't make sense to me. People thought I was crazy when I would tell them about my dreams, and that those dreams would eventually become reality.

We stood in the lake a bit longer as Cyrus released her howl to bring in the end of the day. I gave Asherah a nod before she turned to leave.

Her figure faded into the orange light, then I turned to Seth, who was no longer upset by today's events. His features seemed more relaxed than anything. I smiled and extended my hand to him. "C'mon. We have more clearing to do tomorrow, and after today, we both need a break."

Seth looked down at my hand and interlaced our fingers as he waded back to the shoreline with me in tow.

Without another word, I grabbed my clothes and began to dress, only for him to stop me mid-way and push my back against the tree.

My gaze shot up at Seth. "What was that for?" I asked, but Seth just lifted me into his arms and drop into a portal back home.

Seth immediately stripped off the remnants of his clothing as I held onto him. His lips crashed into mine with a sense of urgency. I wrapped my legs around his torso as he carried me to the couch, setting me down on the edge. He pushed me down and spread my legs with his knees.

I pulled away and cupped his face with my petite hands. "S-S-S-eth?" I stuttered.

"This is my way of apologizing for earlier," he replied, his voice husky.

I smiled lazily at him. "You don't have to apologize, love. There was a huge misunderstanding on my pa—" My words were muffled by his lips against mine.

Seth, please, not now.

His kisses stopped almost immediately as he pulled himself away. "Is everything alright? Am I upsetting you?" Seth asked with a worried tone.

"No, no, I'm fine." I ducked my head shyly. "It's just that it's been a long day, and I want to lie down for a bit and talk first."

"What do you want to talk about?" he asked, seeming eager to get on with it.

I shrugged. "Anything, everything. Whatever is on your mind. It's been six months, and we don't get to talk much."

Seth sighed and extended his hand to me. I placed my hand in his and rose from the couch, and the two of us made our way upstairs and into our room. "Alright, what do you want to know?" he asked as we sat on the bed.

"Well first can I... maybe borrow a shirt?" I fiddled with the blanket, turning my gaze away from him, but he cupped my cheek with his hand.

"Is that even a real question? Of course." he smiled before grabbing the most oversized shirt in the entire closet. I giggled as he slipped it over my head.

"This thing is huge!" I chuckled, slipping my arms through the sleeves.

Seth raised a brow at me. "Oh? I know something else that's big." He winked at me and scooped me back into his arms before settling back into bed.

I snuggled into his chest and let out a long breath. "So, the ritual you mentioned earlier?" I pointed out, only to feel him tense beneath me.

"How did I know you were going to ask about that?" he grumbled.

I shrugged and gazed up at him. "Probably because you mentioned it earlier."

Seth rolled his eyes and rubbed his face. "Uh, yeah, okay. So, here's the thing, Iris. You're going to have to save every bit of energy you can between now and then."

I sat up, never shifting my gaze. "For what? Am I performing this ritual, or are you going to need my energy while you perform it?"

"You're going to be performing it. Your Earth element is going

to revive the Earth's lands and purify the water once we wash the waste away. But there is one problem." He held his index finger up.

"Seth, I don't think I'm ready for that. What am I supposed to do? What am I supposed to say?" I started firing off questions, not giving him a chance to speak.

He pressed his finger against my lips and gave me a stern glare that caused my skin to prickle in goosebumps. "You will know what to do and say when the time is right. Don't stress yourself over this."

I lowered my head and nodded before leaning into him. "So…What's the problem?"

"You have a high chance of not surviving this on your own. But with our soul tie… You have a very small chance," he stated, giving me a tight squeeze. "Don't worry, I have a feeling you're going to do just fine."

I blinked for a moment as I processed this information. My nerves began firing off waves of anxiety. "I—I don't know what to say. I mean… death? Seth, are you serious?"

He sighed loudly. "When have I ever lied about something as serious as this?"

"Well, why can't we start reviving it little bit by little bit?" I asked.

I felt Seth shake his head. "We can't. It must be done all at the same time, and we still have Europe and Asia to clear. So, if I disappear off to the temple, please, for the love of everything sacred, just come with me."

"What?" My head shot up. "You're assuming I'll want to play a damsel in distress, knowing that freaking psycho is out there trying to keep me for himself?"

"We need to get rid of him and Osiris. But we have so much work to do. I know this sounds annoying because I can't trust you to not go running off without me present. Cyrus lost track of you earlier today, and instead we ended up arguing," Seth stated.

I calmly unwrapped his arms from around me and shook my head after I slid from his lap to the hardwood floor. I nonchalantly took his shirt off, dropped it, and gave him my middle finger as I sashayed out of the room. "You want Osiris dead? You got it," I growled under my breath.

I pulled a black dress with a deep V-neck from the closet in the hallway and threw my hair into a half-up half-down hairstyle with a sharpened hairpin. I slipped on a pair of matching sandals and marched out of the door.

As I stomped through the long grass, the hairs on my arms and the back of my neck stood rigid. I stood tall as I spotted a familiar pair of forest-green eyes glowing in the distance. "I'm going to kill this son of a bitch," I muttered to myself.

A sudden gust of wind rushed from behind me, causing me to turn around just as Osiris appeared. I smiled sweetly, needing to coax him into letting me close enough to him to kill him once and for all.

"What would you be doing out here in the dark without your guardian, little Iris?" Osiris asked as he clasped his hands behind his back. He leaned forward as if he were interested in what I had to say.

I seductively grazed my finger across my chest and gave him a yearning look. "Well, after that whole debacle at the lake, I wanted to thank you for telling me about Seth's plan to use me." I giggled.

Iris... You are dancing with fire, Seth's voice echoed in my mind.

I may be dancing with fire, but I control it, I shot back.

I don't think you understand what he can do to you.

And I don't think you understand what I can do to him. But you're going to help me with this, and you don't have a choice in the matter.

Seth growled in my head, *I thought you wanted to rest, but here we go with you running off again. Call for me when you're ready,* he huffed as he left me to do my own bidding.

Osiris cautiously walked in circles around me, as if to size me up. I couldn't help but roll my eyes.

"See something you like?" I asked, peeking over my shoulder at him.

Osiris grunted suspiciously. "It's rather odd that you'd come and search me out, especially after our last encounter."

"All this time, I believed Seth was my one true guardian. But then, after you explained, it seems he wasn't. I took what you said into consideration, " I replied, taking a step towards him. "Six months is a long time to be deceived."

A smirk appeared on Osiris's face as I reached out to stroke his cheek.

"Why not show me what a real God can do?"

He wrapped his arm around my waist and lifted me. "As you wish." Osiris teleported us from the middle of the field to a building outside the Dome.

My heart raced when I looked around to see a familiar space. "Osiris, where are we?" I stuttered.

"Oh, this is my new home since Ra banished me. What, you don't like it?" he asked as he pushed me against the wall, pinning me with his arms.

I let out a harsh breath. *Am I as good as dead? Why did he bring me to this cell? Can I even kill him?* Sliding one hand behind my back, I swirled my finger in circles and focused on his blood. I hoped I could incapacitate him for even a moment so I could rip his heart out or, even better yet, decapitate him.

Sure, I was angry enough at him for even making me doubt Seth and his intentions. And at the same time, Seth had proven to me time and time again that he was my guardian. He was going to protect and love me.

Osiris coughed, loosening his tie as if he were choking. "Iris, what is this?" He coughed again.

I smiled as I reached up to remove my hairpin, releasing my tresses. I gripped the pin like a knife and waited for the perfect moment to strike. "Oh? What do you mean, Osiris? It's a little stuffy in here." I continued to twirl my finger behind my back.

Osiris brought his face closer to mine, causing my breath to hitch. His hand came down to stroke my hair. "Little Iris. Don't play me for a fool."

I wrapped my arms around his neck and pulled him even closer. I positioned the pin behind his back pointed at his heart. "Osiris, I—I want you to…" I lightly moaned as he pressed his body against mine.

My dear. It's time, I sent to Seth.
"Yes? What is it you want?" he growled, cupping my chin.
I smiled maliciously, formed a fist with my free hand, constricted his body with his own blood, and drove the pin into his heart from his back. I pushed the pin all the way through until the point stuck out of his chest. "I want you to die." I gripped him by the back of his neck and squeezed with all my strength, watching the helpless God as he struggled to move and breathe.

Seth appeared behind Osiris and gripped the sides of his head. I smiled at the sight as I released my hold on Osiris while Seth brought the man to his knees.
"I want you to die, Osiris. You're nothing but a threat to me and my people," I shouted at him as Seth stomped on his leg and yanked his head clean from between his shoulders.
Osiris's body fell limp to the floor. I gazed into his eyes during his final moments. "This time, no one will be bringing you back. Not even Isis."
Seth dropped his head against the cold tiled floor and let out a harsh breath and spat. "Fucking imbecile."
I rolled my eyes and held my hand out. The blood from Osiris's open wound came swirling out of his body and into a perfect sphere of dark red spinning in my hand. "Should we put it in a jar?"
"Yea, sure." He dropped into a portal and reappeared with a jar.
"Oh, that was fast." I released my hold on the sphere, and Osiris's blood fell into the vessel after Seth pulled the lid open.
"You tend to say that a lot. If you want I can show you just how fast I really am." He winked.

"Oh lordy, let's not please. This is definitely not the mood."

Seth reached out to me and gestured for me to take his hand. I pursed my lips together as I took hold. A portal opened below us, and we both dropped in and reappeared at home.

My mind began to race, the image of Osiris's face burned into my memory. *What have I done?* "Seth, I think I'm going crazy," I whispered, lowering my gaze to the floor. "I actually enjoyed killing him. Like, it was nothing for me. I'm not sad that he's dead but... I—"

"Iris, don't feel bad. After everything that's happened, he is no longer a threat to you," Seth soothed as he pulled me closer.

She is really able to kill us. Even in our immortal state... I heard Seth's voice in my head.

"It's nice to know how you really feel, Seth," I hissed, turning away to head upstairs to shower. "I smell like blood and sweat and ugh!"

"Here's one problem," Seth grumbled. "He had The Book of Death."

I had forgotten entirely. "I'm just... fucking everything up left and right, huh?" I asked, gazing up at him to gauge his reaction.

Seth looked down at me and chuckled. "Ra can find it. Those are his books, after all." He shrugged as his eyes scanned over me. "Are you hurt?" He jutted his chin at the blood-stains on both of my hands.

I shifted my gaze to look. "This isn't mine. All of it is Osiris's. I made sure that he didn't suspect anything before I—"

"Yeah, I fucking heard everything..." Seth huffed. "Go, get cleaned up," he barked.

I winced at his harsh tone. "Should we maybe have taken his head? You know, so a certain someone doesn't come and try to put him back together?"

Seth raised a brow. "You remember that story, huh?"

I nodded and clasped my hands together. "I do..."

Seth growled and dropped back into a portal, reappearing minutes later with some of Osiris' dismembered body parts. "Let's make sure to burn these. And next time, don't go storming off like that; I don't want you to get hurt. Honestly, I don't know what I'd do if something happened."

"But... You—never mind," I sighed. Not wanting to argue, I continued up the stairs into our master bath and shut the door behind me. I slipped out of the dress and reached over to turn on the standing shower before turning back to the mirror. I stared at myself for a moment. *What else can I do wrong tonight? It's literally one thing after another,* I thought to myself.

Tears brimmed my eyes as I stepped around the frosted glass and into the shower—the realization of what I just did clicking in my mind. I killed a man... I really killed a man. A God, nonetheless.

"It really happened. I let my anger get the best of me," I sniffled. Wiping away my falling tears, I stood with my head leaning against the wall as the streams of water pelted my back.

How could I have pushed myself that hard? I began to doubt my ability to control my emotions, especially at a time like this. *How... Just how? A God... An immortal. Seth is going to hate me.*

A knock came on the door before it opened. I didn't bother to move, since I already knew who it was.

"Are you here to give me another lecture? I'm already punishing myself," I cried.

Seth huffed from behind me, and to my surprise, he approached me. "No, I'm not going to lecture you. But I am going to tell you that I'm proud that you were able to face your fears when it came to Osiris. Just... be careful with your anger."

Sniffling, I brought my hands to cover my face as I continued silently sobbing. "Seth, I don't know what to do, how I should feel right now. My mind is all over the place again."

A tingling sensation ran down my spine. Gasping, I reached back and found that it was Seth's fingertips gently grazing my skin.

"Do you want to know the reason why I've fallen in love with you?" he asked.

I froze for a moment, hesitant to even hear the reason at this point. I nodded.

"It's because you're brave, and you know how to quickly adapt to your environment. You came here from a whole different timeline and yet you're not even fazed by the fact that you don't belong here."

I took a deep breath and slowly exhaled, thinking of my old life and how simple things used to be. "Well, I've always lived my life by enjoying the simple things. Complaining about something I cannot change wouldn't help my situation at all—it'd just stress me out and nothing good ever comes from that." I turned around to face him.

"That is a great ideology to live by." Seth leaned down and kissed my forehead and smiled. "I have a confession…"

I raised a brow at him as his nervous energy pushed itself onto me. "And what would that be?" I stepped into the steady stream of water.

"You're the only one who's been able to fulfill me. Even in this short amount of time together."

My heart swelled at his words. *Seth feels fulfilled… by me?* "How… Do I fulfill you?"

"We will talk about that at a later time."

I anticipated his next move as his hands glided down my hips. His hooded eyes glinted with lust. "You know, it's hard to control these urges with you," he said as his lips captured mine.

Our passion brought the house to life.

Chapter 18: Traveling Wonders

Seth

I couldn't keep my hands off of her. Throughout the evening and into the black of night, until sunrise, our passion for each other danced. Neither one of us slept a wink, but to my surprise, Iris was full of life and energy, ready to take on the day.

I had planned to visit the temple to speak with Portù and see his progress of the revival ritual. My only setback was that the book of death was still missing. Ra could sense it outside of the Dome somewhere in Eastern Asia, China, and then homed in on its location in Beijing.

Iris was geared up and ready to hit the city. I stood and watched as she quickly dressed herself, tying back her hair in a low, braided ponytail. I waited patiently, shirtless, my gaze trailed from her tiny feet to the nape of her neck. Snapping myself out of my daze, I slipped into my black tee.

The need to capture each and every moment with her pushed through my mind and images of her burned into my memory. At this pace, the ritual would take place in the next couple of weeks. That was assuming we recovered the book, of course.

"Seth, is something wrong? I'm getting an uneasy feeling, and these emotions aren't mine," Iris called over to me.

I blinked a few times to regain my focus. "It's nothing."

She stopped and turned to face me. Her hands were still intertwined with her long, snow-white strands. "Well, where are we headed?"

My lip flattened into a straight line. "Beijing."

Her eyes widened, and her lips parted. Something swirled in the back of her mind as if a secret had been unlocked. I couldn't help but wonder what had caused her to stiffen, as fear transformed her playful expression, this caused my skin to prickle with goosebumps.

"Is there something wrong? Now I'm getting an uneasy feeling from you." I took a step toward Iris, only for her to step back.

Iris brought her hand to her chest, and her breath quickened. "You can't take me back there... Seth, please don't."

What the hell? My heart pounded in my chest as her fearful emotions pushed into my veins. My muscles tensed, and panic rose. *Why is she afraid?*

I quickly closed the space between us and wrapped my arms around her tiny frame. "Did you remember something about that place? Have you been there before?" I asked as I rubbed her back.

Iris

The warmth of Seth's body against mine while he held me gave me a sense of safety. The panic, anxiety, anger, and confusion flooded my veins at the mention of Beijing, but why?

Something in the back of my mind snapped as images of my arrival here came flooding in like the Tsunami I tamed all those years ago. The memory played out in the back of my mind.

Twelve years prior

I recalled the sound of children sloshing across the dampened white sands, the clear ocean water before me as I sat in my beach chair with my giant umbrella and a good book in my hands. It was a little chilly for just my bikini, so I wore a pair of white capri pants and a lace shawl.

The crashing of the waves against the shore was music to my ears as I flipped through pages of the newest addition to my ever-growing collection: *McKenna's Crossing*. I thumbed through a few pages before a shout interrupted me. Thinking it was someone calling for their spouse or child, I didn't skip a beat and continued reading.

I felt something tug at my feet and peeked over my book, only to find nothing. "Hmm? That's weird." I shrugged off the feeling and adjusted my feet.

"Lady! Lady! You gotta get out of here!" a man shouted at me.

I raised my eyebrow, turned to look at the cause of the ruckus, and found he was pointing towards the receding waterline. I paused for a moment and turned to look in the direction, only to find myself calm, relaxed, and unmoving.

"Iris," a distant voice called out to me.

"Lady, c'mon, there's a tsunami coming!" someone else shouted at me.

Something clicked in my chest. I brought my hand up to rub the sore spot, then faced the swell that was rapidly approaching the shore. I didn't skip a beat, my hand raised on its own. With a simple "stop" gesture, my hand then made a tilting motion as if I were pushing the wave back. The wave mimicked my hand motion and quickly leveled back to a calm ocean.

I turned my eyes back to my book and continued reading as everyone around me stood gawking at the sight in confusion. Silence fell upon the beach that day, and I had not the slightest clue as to what these people thought about me. At that point, I didn't give it much thought, until an invisible web pulled me into the water. Kicking and screaming, I tried to break free, only to plunge deep into the Pacific.

I held my breath as best I could, terrified hat I was indeed going to drown. My eyes frantically searched the area around me, only to realize I was still breathing. *Wait? How could that be? I'm not a mermaid.*

What the hell? I thought to myself as I continued to descend to the ocean floor.

A dog-like shadow figure appeared before me. "Finally found you." Its deep, ethereal tone reverberated in the back of my mind.

My gaze shot straight to what looked to be some sort of portal. I didn't fight against the pull, instead I closed my eyes as my body disappeared into it, only to reappear on another shore. My muscles ached, my head spun, and my heart throbbed when I gasped for air, knowing damn well I was breathing under water not too long before.

"Where the hell am I?" I coughed, scanning the area with my blurred vision. The bile in my stomach rose along with a wave of nausea. With a fist full of sand, I pushed with all of my remaining strength to sit up, only to expel the contents of my stomach in a puddle beside me before collapsing face-first into the sand.

My mind swirled, and anxiety flooded my heart, pumping its venom through my veins. "Where am I? What happened?" I weakly mumbled.
The sound of approaching footsteps in the sand caused my eyes to shift upward. A man stood before me with his hands in his pockets. A smirk played upon his lips. "So, the rumors were true."
I let out a harsh breath before losing consciousness.

The steady beeping of a machine brought me back to reality. *Did I remember that correctly? I was pulled into the water... only to resurface somewhere else.*

Something inside of me pushed to the surface. "Give it time. He will find you." A woman's voice calmed me as the shuffling of feet surrounded me and pandemonium broke out.

I sensed multiple people around me, but I couldn't figure out what on earth was going on. Their multiple cries for help and disoriented panic arose.

"What's going on?" I began to panic like everyone around me, but I couldn't move. The beeping of the machine rose to match my rapid heartrate.

"What's going on?" a voice sounded from what I believed was an intercom.

The men around me began explaining that my cognitive function was returning. Their voices were laced with fear. My ears searched for a focal point for whomever was in charge of whatever was going on.

"We need to move her from this facility," a voice stated.

"But, Ian, Beijing is the most protected facility in the world. Where would we move her?" another voice replied.

"Somewhere, anywhere. This facility is not protected against the Gods, and they will come looking."

I slowly clenched my fist. My body felt as if it were taken over, possessed by something as a smile forced its way onto my lips. The gentle lapping of water filled the room. The muffled cries of those who were around me brought me a sense of peace and the noises around me stopped.

The water receded, and the air was still. I lay there waiting for something to come next, only to hear myself speak when I sat up, my eyes locked onto the man I had seen on the shore.

"Oh, Captain. You know you won't be able to contain me. Not at this rate." An evil grin worked
its way across my lips.

Captain? How the hell? This isn't my voice! Who the hell is speaking? A hissing sound poured into my ears as the room filled with

145

smoke moments later. My eyes became heavy and I fell back into the blackness of sleep.

A man's voice boomed over me when I finally came to. I still had no idea where I was, but now I was strapped to a bed and inside of what sounded like a helicopter. The spinning blades cut through the air with each turn, burning my ears. The smell lingering in the air scorched my nasal passages. *What the...?*

"Sir! It's that thing again!" a man shouted.
"Get her out of here! Now!" another replied as a loud roar erupted from below me.
Over time, I felt as if I were in a dream-like state. I wasn't aware of the chaos that erupted around me. Waking and sleeping, waking and sleeping. Those were the cycles I fell in and out of, only to be left behind in a shithole of a glass cell filled with the bodies of the guards and those who sought me out when I met my rescuer.
The man I came to love and adore.

Seth.

His voice called to me from the present moment. "Iris? Are you okay? You're shaking." I gazed up and saw Seth. I wrapped my arms around myself and whimpered as my eyes searched the room for something, anything to anchor myself.

The truth? I was scared beyond anything.

I shut my eyes and shook my head. "I remember. I remember everything." I sucked in a heavy breath.

"What do you remember?" Seth asked, a gentle hand on my shoulder.

I held myself tightly to stop the shaking. "Ian. The man's name is Ian. He moved me around, from what I could gather during the little time I was awake."

"I triggered your wake response every time I neared your location. They moved you as soon as they were able to sense my presence," he growled.

"And they did that for twelve whole fucking years," I whispered. "You really did care. You weren't going to leave me to die or to become their experiment. You actually found me." Tears formed and fell as I gazed up at him, clutching my chest.

"I wasn't given much choice in the matter, but if I had known what I do now, I would have stopped at nothing. If I had to do it all again, I would have gotten to you sooner," he said, soothing me with his voice. "C'mon, we gotta get going. It's going to be a hell of a ride if we are going to get this ritual ready in time."

I sighed heavily and turned to the mirror. I gave myself a once-over, wiping the spilled tears from my cheek, and turned back to Seth. "Let's go get that book back," I said with a nod.

Seth smiled and extended his hand. I took it without hesitation, and we both dropped into a portal, reappearing just outside of the building where it all began.

Beside the small gusts of wind that swirled around us, the area was quiet, like you could hear a fly fart, quiet. I quickly scanned the open space and then shifted my gaze toward Seth.

"Where is everyone?" I asked.

He shrugged. "Better for it to be quiet than to have to waste my energy killing those damn things."

As if he'd spoken of the devil, a single slow round of applause sounded from behind us, causing the both of us to spin around.

"Ian," I whispered.

An evil grin was painted across his face as he stopped clapping. "My dear princess, you've returned home."

His voice sent a chill up my spine, but I held my ground. I couldn't give this lowlife the satisfaction of seeing that I feared him.

"So, you remembered where you came from!" He smirked.

I took a step towards him with my hand outstretched. "Does the objective remain the same?" I asked.

He simply nodded and turned around to walk back into the building. "It does, princess."

"Then you die today," Seth growled, cutting me off.
 My insides screamed. Why on Earth would someone not accept the fact that all of us that sought refuge in the Dome, including me, were different? I pushed back my fear and shouted with clenched fists. "How could you be willing to murder the entire human race just to expose us? What did we ever do to you?"
"What hasn't your kind done? They promised to bring peace to this planet, and all they did was start a war," he sneered as he whipped back around to face us.

Seth instinctively stepped in front of me, guns drawn. "I'd stop right there if I were you."

Ian smirked. "Or what, Seth? You're gonna shoot me?" He began to walk toward us.

"You know what? This might be more entertaining using my own two fists," Seth shot back with a smirk.

I sighed loudly and stepped back. *I'm going to search the area for the book. Keep him busy.*

Don't get yourself into trouble.

Trouble will find me eventually. I can handle myself.

You know where to find me. I'll be close by with this idiot.

148

With that, I slowly backed away. Seth grabbed Ian as he charged him and dropped into a portal, disappearing from my line of sight.

I turned around and scanned the buildings before me and groaned. "Well, here goes nothing." I took off running and focused my senses on the book.

Ra, can you assist me with this?

Yes, child, I can do that.
Are you sure it's the Book of Life that's missing, and not the Book of the Dead?
It's the book of life; I'm sure of it.

Well, the book that is missing is black.
A pause. *Are you sure?*
I'm positive, Ra. The one Seth had was gold. That's the book of life, is it not?
Another pause. *How did I miss that?*
Good question. Now tell me where the hell I need to go to find the book of the dead. I don't want to be here any longer than I have to.
Little one, you don't need to command me to get something done.
I know. I just don't want to argue right now. I want to go home as soon as possible. Please, just help me find this book.
As I ran, the groaning and crunching of rocks came from behind a building just a few yards ahead of me. My heart throbbed in my ears as anxiety fluttered in my stomach. I knew they sensed my presence, so I quickly looked around for a hiding spot.

My gaze scanned the destruction around me and landed on a burned SUV. The doors were missing, and bits of glass were mixed in with the gravel around it. A destroyed vehicle, perfect. I ran behind it, crouched, and peeked around the corner, trembling slightly, to see a half a dozen soulless with their noses in the air as if they were attempting to catch my scent. I couldn't sit there long; their crunching footsteps closed in on my poor hiding spot. I froze in fear, not having any other plans for where the hell I was to go.

T.K. MOORE

Shit, I thought as my brain swirled around the ideas of an escape route. *Oh God, how could I forget?* I snapped my fingers, and a wall of stone shot up from the ground a foot to the side of the vehicle, giving me enough cover to advance without being seen. I slowly moved behind it so I wouldn't make too much noise. *Darn these boots!* I thought as my combat boots impacted loudly against the rocks with each step.

A low growl rumbled behind me. I slowly turned around to see what once had been a man in his late thirties standing behind me. His eyes were white, and his ripped flesh hung around his neck and arm. I swallowed hard and took a deep breath, my brain screaming as my body refused to move.

The man growled at me and charged. I threw my hand up and sent him flying into the building across the abandoned street. The other soulless heard the commotion and came running to the source. I jumped to my feet and took off toward a building that seemed as if it hadn't been affected by the destruction surrounding it.

Reaching for my water pouch, I spun around as soon as I had put enough distance between me and the soulless. In a smooth motion, I popped the cap and poured the water out. I willed the water to stop midair, and the cascading droplets took the shape of spears. Once they were close enough, I shot each of the pursuing soulless down, the icy spears penetrating their skulls. I took off running toward the building again.

Seth, are you okay?

I'm fine. Are you all right?

I checked myself over. *For the most part, yeah.*

What the fuck is that supposed to mean?

Don't start that with me right now. I'm currently scouting this building. I'll check back in a few.

Wait—

150

I searched the perimeter of the building and found a single windowless steel door and reached for the handle. To my dismay, the door was locked. I hesitated for a moment, wondering about traps and what I might find before I snapped my finger. A solid piece of Earth shot up from under the door, crushing it against its frame. Once the stone wall receded, the now accordion door hit the ground with a loud bang.

The beeping of machines and robotic whirring zoomed overhead. I quickly moved into the building and took refuge behind a stack of tin boxes. "What the hell is this place?" I peeked from behind the boxes and didn't see or hear any other signs of life.

Iris, where are you? Seth sounded almost frantic— the way he always did when I wasn't where he expected me to be.

In a... factory of some sort?

What?

You gotta come see this.

I glanced around again. I was standing on a platform above rows of mechanical arms. I watched them as they zoom upward, shift, then dropped down onto something. My curiosity was piqued, and I wandered over to the edge. My jaw dropped when my eyes landed on what looked to be artificial... wombs?

My hands shook. I placed them on the railing as my gaze traveled further down. There were taller, much bigger glass incubators for what looked like adults, and even a few smaller ones for teenagers, children, and toddlers.

"This... This isn't real. This can't be real." I gripped the sides of my head and shut my eyes. The images of babies, children, and even adults filling these tanks still flooded my mind.

The crumpled metal scraped across the ground as the hall echoed with quickened footsteps. I didn't even bother to look up. I dropped to a crouched position and shook my head. If the person approaching me was Ian, I guessed I was as good as dead. The horror before me had shaken my very soul; the overwhelming disgust paralyzed me.

"Iris? Are you— What in the…"

I released the grip on my hair and shifted my gaze upward at the sound of Seth's voice. "This is horrible. This place is an absolute hell." My voice shook.

"That bastard wasn't kidding when he said he had clones of every pure human." Seth grabbed the railing and peered over the edge. "That drop goes into the Earth. Is that how he's keeping them alive?"

I reached up and grabbed the railing with one hand and Seth's pants leg with the other. My legs wavered, making it difficult to stand. "Let's get the fucking book and get the hell out of here, please," I begged.

Seth wrapped his arm around my waist and lifted me into his arms, gently squeezing. "This is too much for you to bear, isn't it, Iris?"

I tucked my head into his chest. "Where is Ian?" I asked in a low tone.

Seth turned and began walking. "He's outside— unconscious, but alive still. We may need to question him."

I grabbed Seth's shirt and let out a harsh breath. "No, why is he still alive? How is he still alive? He's human."

Seth scoffed. "No. No, he isn't. This entire war was basically for nothing. He thought humans were superior to us."

I shook my head. "This is all crazy. Everything is just—" I let out a long breath to settle my raging nerves. A presence lingered in the back of my awareness, and I listened for its voice.

The book is in that building. Not too far ahead of you two now.

Thank you, Ra.

Hurry up and get out of there

We're trying, I acknowledged. *I'm going to burn this shithole to the ground before we leave.*

I shifted my gaze toward Seth and pointed to the other side of the building. "It's somewhere over there."

Chapter 19: Atlas

Seth

I turned my gaze to the direction that Iris was pointing in. I assumed she had received the directions from Ra.

"You should wait outside. I don't know what's lurking around here, so let me get this done and then we can burn this place to the ground."

Iris looked at me and nodded as she wiped a stray tear that had fallen from her beautiful eyes. "I'll be just outside, then." She turned to walk away, and I couldn't help but stare at her as her figure disappeared.

My heart broke seeing her reaction to this facility. The thoughts running through her mind were going to put her in a catatonic state when we got back.

I furrowed my brow, turning in the direction Iris had pointed out and simply leapt from one end to the other with ease as the low, whirring hums of the machines shifted below.

"This is really a hellhole. Why did he do this to those humans?" I shook my head as I reached for the door handle.

The building shook for a brief moment. A familiar scream followed the rumbling. "Seth!"

I spun around and leapt back outside to find Iris on the ground pointing off into the distance. I turned my head in the direction she

154

indicated. My lips parted as my eyes widened. "What the fuck?" I muttered to myself.

"Seth, what the hell are those things!" she screamed again, causing the surface of the Earth to shake.

Off in the distance, the clouds we had just cleared were rolling back in. I blinked and looked closer. No, it was the flapping of wings, and those bastards were headed straight for us.

Ian's groans pulled my focus off of the Avians and onto him. "Oh, you're fucking awake now, huh?" I snapped.

Ian groaned as he gripped the sides of his head. "What the hell did you do to me?"

I rolled my eyes at Ian and offered Iris my hand. "Come."

A familiar warmth enveloped my hand as Iris gripped me with both of hers and pulled herself up off the ground. My heart throbbed when that warmth rushed through me.

"Ian, I think they're here for you." I jutted my chin at the Avians, who landed a few hundred yards behind him. The man who stood out the most was an older acquaintance. His skin was blue and riddled in patches of feathers and he had a beak in place of his lips. I didn't realize he was back on Earth. But I wasn't surprised he had returned for such an occasion.

"Atlas." I gave him a nod as he tucked his wings in. I watched carefully as the others followed suit.

"Seth. What the hell have you gotten yourself into this time that required me to come back down to this… " He took a quick look around, seeming startled at the tragic desolation of the wasteland surrounding us. "Well, what the hell happened here?" he asked with a raised brow.

I glanced down at Iris, then back to Atlas. "You're going to have to ask that asshole." I tilted my brow in Ian's direction. "And you might want to inform him that he's not actually what he thinks he is."

I watched as Atlas's gaze shifted to Iris. A smile formed at the corners of his beak. "And you must be what the commotion is all about." He bowed his head. "I'm Atlas, of the Avian Starseeds, and you are Miss Iris, if I'm correct?"

"Yes, she was sent here from the other timeline to save us all," I replied for her.

"Ah, I see. Well, you're quite fond of this one. I can see it in your eyes." Atlas shifted his gaze back to me. "Seth, I need to know what the hell happened here."

"Ian here destroyed the entire human race. Now, he's got a factory full of clones and the book of the dead." I jabbed my thumb toward the building.
Atlas hissed at the thought. "Let's see what terror this foolish nephew of mine has brought upon you all, shall we?" He gestured for us to take a walk.

Did I hear that right? Is Ian his nephew? I thought.

You can't be serious?

He said it, not me.

My grip on Iris tightened for a moment, causing Atlas to look down at our joined hands. "Don't worry, I brought enough men to take care of Ian while we go retrieve that precious book of yours, Seth. Come, we have much to discuss about Ian's troublesome behavior." He sent a hiss in Ian's direction.

I nodded and looked down at Iris. "I'll be quick. That building can't take another one of your Earthquakes right now, and we really need that book, so… watch the screams." I leaned down and kissed the top of her head.

She sighed and slouched her shoulders. "I'll do my best not to scream," she mocked, crossing her arms. Iris pointed to the trio in front of her. "Can I at least know who these men are? I don't like being rude."

"Oh, now you have manners?" I snickered and pointed to the three Avians in front, closest to her. "That one is Indigo, yes like the color. The one beside him is Garrett, plain name, I know. And that one behind those two is Yari."

Iris nudged me with her tiny elbow and huffed. "I can be myself with you, that's why," she muttered before releasing my hand.

I love you.

Iris instantly smiled and stuck her tongue out at me. *I love you, too, you big oaf.*

I'll be back. Don't kill Ian... yet.

Fine, fine, I won't. I'll start burning the other buildings around here to keep myself occupied.

I grinned, already turning toward the facility again. The ignition of fire whooshed behind me. "Atta girl," I whispered to myself.

As Atlas and I entered the facility, his jaw dropped, a shriek leaving his throat. "Seth, what on Earth is going on in here?" he asked as he frantically searched the building. "What did Ian do?" he shouted.

I plugged my ear with my finger for a moment and scrunched my face. "I fucking told you, this idiot killed all of the humans and made clones. He's growing them. I don't know if he's been able to bring back their souls."

Atlas pinched the bridge of his nose and let out a long breath, "Yep. I'm gonna kill him. That's it, no more chances for him. We will make sure to do a better job of following his soul after we kill him this time..."

I raised my brow as I unplugged my ear. "What? What do you mean no more chances? He's done this before? Killing him will make his soul harder to track. Why not just use him as an eternal punching bag?"

Atlas nodded. "Yeah, what the hell did you think happened to Mars? And Neptune?"

"He destroyed the atmosphere. Froze it over. And Mars, he turned into a desert... Wait, that was him?" I facepalmed. *How did I miss that?* "So his real name is—"

"Yep, and we don't ever speak that name anymore, trust me. He's already long forgotten it. Last thing we need is Armageddon," he replied.

"So, what really happened with this idiot?" I placed a hand on the railing, leaning against it.

Atlas ran a hand through his feathery head and sighed. "In another lifetime, Ian had just finished destroying Mars. The Avian council needed him to stand trial for his crimes, but his parents refused to tell us where he was and I couldn't find him either. The council got antsy and ordered them to be killed."

Killed? Extreme but understandable. "That's fucked up, Atlas. But you guys have your laws and we have ours and I am not going to meddle in your political affairs, as I have my own to deal with."

Atlas nodded his head in agreement and clicked his beak. "Well—"

"Fuck, let's get this book and get the hell out of here."

"Yeah. I don't want to look at these poor fleshy robots anymore," he hissed as he quickly scanned the room.

I stalked off toward a series of doors on the other side of the platform. Kicking each door down one by one, I found more and more of Ian's crazy experiments. It wasn't just humans he was growing: there were clones of fairies, dragons, and other creatures of the sort who had been taking refuge in the Dome.

As Atlas and I approached the final unopened door, I stepped back and kicked it down with ease, sending it flying off its hinges. My eyes scanned the room and stopped when they found what they were looking for. The book of the dead, sitting on a table in the corner covered in dust.

Granted it's been months since the damned book went missing, but why hasn't he used it yet? I thought as I walked over and snatched a note off of the table as Atlas stopped in the doorway, leaning against the post.

My muscles tensed when an overwhelming fear of death washed over me. "This… is my revival ritual… But for these clones. Did Osiris give this to him?" I crumpled the paper.

I was getting tired of these games, and we needed to get the hell out of Beijing before Iris did something she'd regret. I could almost hear the heartbeats of those things down in the incubation chambers. I cringed, hoping they didn't have souls.

A loud crack echoed through the facility as the ground shifted below us. Smoke poured in, filling the air.

"Iris!" I shouted, and I snatched the book off of the table and bolted out of there with Atlas not far behind.

Once out of the building, my eyes searched for Iris, only to realize she was standing in the center of a raging fire she had started around the facility and nearby buildings. My jaw dropped as my gaze trailed to her face.

A red glowing light appeared on her skin just above her chin. Her fire element had fully awakened, and that was going to be bad news if she couldn't control it.

Chapter 20: Let It Burn

Iris

The inferno I created was rapidly growing with each passing minute. I smiled at the dancing flames and continued on while my Avian trio stood guard.

I could feel my soul come to life as I danced alongside the fire. The images of the inside of the facility faded. Oh, it was a beautiful sight indeed. Giggling, I waved my arm and commanded the stream of flame to the back of the facility Seth and Atlas had disappeared into.

"Iris, you must stop this! You'll kill them!" Ian shouted at me only for Garret to restrain him as he attempted to lunge at me.

"I can't kill what isn't alive! And you were the one who started this! Do they have their souls? Are they just beings of flesh being grown?" I shouted back. "The only abomination here is you! They never would have been here if you didn't— " My anger got the best of me. I couldn't sit back and let this maniac believe he was above everyone else. I clenched my fist and turned to face him.

"Ian, if you had never done this shit in the first place, I wouldn't fucking be here. This timeline would have been safe, and everyone would still be alive." I stomped up to him and grabbed the front of his shirt as he stared back at me with fear in his eyes. "You fucking did this. You're responsible for the deaths of those clones, not me!" I screamed.

160

The forceful wind that left my lips peeled away at Ian's flesh, revealing what looked to be a second layer of skin. The ground shook for a moment as crunching footsteps raced behind me.

I shoved Ian away from me, a look upon my face of disgust when I scanned over his face. "You... You're not even human, either!" I shrieked, causing the Earth to quake once more.

"That's what I was coming to tell you..." Atlas' voice pulled me from my anger.

"What?" I craned my neck at him.

Atlas took a step back as he kept my gaze. "He isn't human. He's just like us, actually. He's my nephew and has been on the run from us since he destroyed not one, but two, I think maybe three planets. His parents wouldn't give him up and instead of standing trial, the council ordered— "

I bit my lower lip and brought my hand up to silence Atlas. I curled all of my fingers but one and slowly turned to gaze toward Seth. Wrath and malice painted my face, and I knew that if I opened my mouth I would cause the world to crumble into dust with just the scream that was begging to be released from within me.

Talk to me.

I'm going to murder this son of a bitch. Get him out of my face before I destroy everything all over again.

Could you do me a favor?

I narrowed my eyes at Seth. *What?*

Breathe... You're turning blue.

I stopped and blinked, releasing a long breath. I rolled my eyes and stomped off to finish burning everything down to the ground. I looked behind me and watched as Garrett and Yari restrained Ian. Atlas

161

cranked his fist back and issued a brutal beat down. Ian's grunts and groans were like music to my ears with each strike that landed on his body.

I smiled and continued into the flames while they engulfed the surrounding buildings. "This world is on fiyah!" I sang from the top of my lungs as I commanded the flames to jump from building to building, enveloping everything in its path, including the cloning factory.

I wish we had s'mores.

What the fuck is that?

You— you've never had a s'more?

No, what the fuck kind of thing is that?

It's delicious!

It sounds stupid.

One day, when things are restored, I will show you the greatness of chocolate and marshmallows with graham crackers.

Okay... Sounds like a deal.
I chuckled to myself as I stood staring into the blaze. "You, my darling, are beautiful." I reached out and scooped a dancing flame into my hand. I twirled the flame around my hand with delight and spun around. The flame followed, eventually encircling me, and shifted into a massive tornado with me as its eye.

My mind was lost to its beauty as I shut my eyes and pirouetted in the center to the beat of my own song. My body and soul were enticed by the flame, my hands waving in the air and seductively sending gouts of fire in various directions. Sparks and explosions blazed, the building crumbling beneath the ravaging flames.

A familiar sensation tugged at my heart when my core ignited. My breath quickened, and my mind raced as I thought about Seth and our intimate moments together.

"Iris!" Seth's voice shouted for me.

I snapped out of my trance, causing the surrounding fire and the flaming tornado to die down from my lack of focus. I slowly raised my eyelids, gazing in his direction with lust-filled eyes.

"Mm? Yes?" I slurred in pleasure.

Seth stalked toward me as if he was angered by my actions. I stood frozen awaiting his verbal discipline, only to be scooped into his arms.

His gaze scanned over my body, checking for something I didn't quite understand.

"Are you all right?" Panic laced his tone.

I blinked and looked down at my hands, then glanced back at him. "I'm fine. Did something happen?" I gazed to my left then right. The buildings that had once stood surrounding us were no more. I had reduced them to piles of soot.

Seth released a sigh of relief and pressed my head to his chest. "You have to stop playing with fire. You're going to hurt yourself."

"Seth, I am fire. Those flames couldn't hurt me if they tried," I replied, gripping his Kevlar. I pressed my hand to my stomach as a tingling sensation ran across my lower half, eventually landing between my legs. "Seth," I panted. "This fucking feeling is back." I tucked my head into his chest and released a muffled cry.

"Shit," he muttered, turning around. "Atlas, can you handle it from here?" he asked.

"Sure can. Is she gonna be alright?" Worry laced his tone.

163

I waved Atlas off as another wave hit me, causing my muscles to tense. A moan escaped my lips and I crossed my legs, squeezing my thighs together. "Seth, we gotta go," I urged. "We can't do this in front of them."

Seth leaned down and whispered, "We could if you wanted to make Ian jealous."

I growled. "Unless you want to walk around with blue balls, I suggest we go," I replied through gritted teeth.

Seth raised a brow. "Oh, you're not only rude, but heartless, too huh?" he chuckled. "Atlas, bring Ian to Ra. He's in the Dome. Take the book back with you, and I'll meet up with you guys, uh… tomorrow."

"You got it." Atlas replied, grabbing Ian's unconscious, bloodied body, and the flock took off into the skies.

Seth opened a portal home and dropped right in. We appeared in our room. Setting me down on the bed, I rolled onto my side, clutching my stomach as my labia throbbed. I was aching for a release.

"Iris, look at me," his husky tone commanded.

I released my hold on my stomach and rolled over, ignoring the ever-growing fire within me. I sat up and gazed into his emerald eyes as I began pulling off my own gear, without ever breaking eye contact.

A low growl escaped his lips while I stripped from my clothing. I rose from the bed to remove the last pieces of fabric that restricted my body before approaching him with haste.

Seth reached down and lifted me into his arms; I wrapped my legs around his waist and clutched onto him. Our lips met and we savored one another with a sense of urgency. His hands gripped my thighs as he swiftly inserted himself into my slit. My nails clawed at his chest and my muffled moans were answered with an ethereal growl of pleasure.

Wrapping my arm around his neck, I lifted myself just enough to leave the tip inserted. I nipped his bottom lip, asking permission for entry, which was granted and welcomed. I purred as Seth ran the tip of his fingers across my thighs leading up to my backside and up to my sides.

I wiggled my hips at him and giggled. Teasing the poor beast would surely earn me a long night of pleasure mixed with pain. Gazing at Seth with lust-filled eyes, I awaited his response.

"You shouldn't do that." His husky tone made me melt into his arms.

"Oh? Or else what, my love?" I replied seductively. I pulled myself up to his neck and kissed a trail from his collarbone to the underside of his ear. I nipped at his lobe and whispered, "I'm all yours."
"Little love, are you so sure you want to test me?" The vibrations of his voice sent a sensual shiver down my spine. A low moan escaped my lips with a rushed breath.

Seth stepped closer to the edge of the bed and laid me down. My legs loosened from around his waist as his lips captured mine in passion. I gave him the opportunity to maneuver his hand between my thighs, and his fingers graze over my bud, causing me to shudder, releasing a muffled moan.

He chuckled against my lips grabbed my wrists, and held them above my head with one hand while he inserted two fingers into my throbbing folds with the other. I arched my back in response when I tried to pull myself free.

I huffed and panted as Seth pulled away from me, licking my juices from his fingers, his eyes raked over my body, and mine followed suit with his own. A sudden yet gentle tug pulled me away from the edge of the bed toward the top.

"Who's teasing now?" I raised a brow at him, biting my bottom lip when my eyes landed on his throbbing erection.

Beads of precum formed at the head of his member as it twitched. I couldn't help but lick my lips at the thought of my mouth around him. My gaze shot back up at Seth, a smirk played across his lips.

"You're really dancing with the devil, dear." He lowered himself between my legs, and his thumb massaged my bud while he rubbed the head of his member against my entrance.

My breath caught in my lungs as a wave of ecstasy coursed through me. My mind swirled as his pace picked up. The knot in my core began to burn with a fury. Struggling and pulling against his grasp, I let out a shaky breath when he removed his hands from between my legs.

"S-Seth, why did y-you stop?" I stumbled over my words when our gazes locked. My body trembled below him as my legs shifted, my body ached for more.

His eyes grew darker, his grip on my wrists loosened when he reached for my waist and flipped me onto my stomach. I gripped the sheets, stunned by the sudden movement only to feel Seth position himself between my legs and rub the head of his member between my folds.

I tilted my head up and watched Seth lick his lips. "You truly are a beautiful being, Iris," he growled in a low tone as he thrusted into me from head to base.

A loud moan escaped from my lungs in a sing-song tone to Seth's ears, earning me an ethereal hiss of sensual pleasure. My toes curled and I reached for a pillow to muffle my screams, and Seth's hand gripped mine as he pulled me into his lap. I huffed, panted and moaned with each thrust, my backside bouncing against him.

Every thickened inch massaged my insides with a sense of urgency, my body responded by clenching around him. I spasmed as Seth slid his hand down my torso and between my legs.

"Oh!" I squeaked when his fingers worked their magic on my bud. I grabbed at his hand in an attempt to pull him away, only for him to growl at me. With his free hand, he grabbed my arm and pulled it behind me, holding me in place.

Don't pull away now, love. You asked for this.

But I'm going to cum soon. I didn't want this night to die down too soon.

Oh, you think this is the only round? Your body is literally begging for this right now. I'm going to bury myself in you all night long.

The constant stimulation pushed my body over the edge as my orgasm washed over me. I came undone in Seth's arms with a chorus of moans and whimpers.

I fell forward only to be pulled back by Seth as he cradled my head with one arm and used his other to maneuver my legs from around his hips.

"Th-that… What was that?" Lights flashed before my eyes as I stared off in a daze.

"It was exactly what you wanted, and I'm nowhere near done with you, little love." He chuckled, kissing a trail from my lower back up to my neck. I purred and whimpered against his touch.

The fire in my core continued to burn. How much longer would I need this?

My oh my is my world on fire or what?

Chapter 21: You Aren't Human

Seth

A few days passed, and Iris had me all to herself. I damn near forgot about the world and its troubles.

Will you two cut it out? Everyone is getting annoyed with you two, and frankly the world isn't going to save itself.

Ra, shut up. You're ruining my mood. I was headed your way, since Iris is asleep finally.

Wait, what do you mean finally?

Well, that fire inside of her finally died down.

Oh my. Granted, Seth, I know what you're capable of, but did you not bring this upon her?

I know what I brought but, uh, no. This all started after she took out China... It wasn't just Beijing, but all of China was in ashes by the time we left.

That's impressive.

You're telling me. She was dancing in the center of a fucking fire tornado.

Well, Atlas is still here, and Ian is unconscious again. You need to hurry over before Atlas loses his patience.

I'll be there; just let me get dressed.

You'd better shower first. I know what you smell like right now, and it's not inviting at all.

Oh, trust me, I know. I wanted to flaunt it.

Seth...

I'm fucking kidding, Ra. I'll be there in a little while.

I rolled my eyes before turning my gaze to my sleeping love beside me. Smiling, I managed to maneuver my arm from under her and leaned down and kissed her forehead. She let out a sleepy moan, tucked her head even deeper into the pillow, and continued to sleep.

Oh, she's going to be out for a while, I thought as I slowly and stealthily slipped out of bed and headed toward the bathroom to get cleaned up.

With a grin plastered on my face, I quickly showered and dressed before dropping into a portal to Ra's holding facility.

The lights flickered above the cell containing the royally confused Avian. I took a quick glance around, as I hadn't stepped foot in this room prior to today. I scrunched my nose at the smell. The stench of putrefied flesh and death invaded my senses; it was atrocious,

"So, what has he said since the other day?" I asked Atlas as I approached. I unbuttoned my cuffs and rolled up my sleeves.

"Well, if you had been here, you would have been able to hear it for yourself," Atlas retorted, crossing his arms over his chest.

I narrowed my eyes at him. "Well, you already know what I was doing, so let's just skip to the end of this."

"Ha, I'll say." Atlas shook his head at me as he chuckled.

"Don't start that shit. You know how an elemental can get, especially with fire," I grumbled at him before shifting my gaze to Ian, whose widened eyes were focused on the ground as if he was in shock.

Ian was covered in bruises and there were open cuts on the surface of his human flesh. His blue complexion and flattened feathers peeked out from behind it. I wondered how he had lived so long without giving us a clue as to who he truly was.

"Ian, I have a few questions for you. You've got two choices, and that's really about it." I placed my hands on my hips and awaited his answer. Honestly, I didn't think he would answer at this point.

His gaze shot up from the floor and froze halfway up my torso. "I've already unleashed my army. That factory wasn't the only one I had." He cackled like a maniac, pulling against his restraints.

My eyes widened as they volleyed between Ra and Atlas. "What the fuck did he just say?" I shouted. Clenching my fists, I cranked my arm back and grabbed the collar of his torn shirt. "What do you mean you've already--"

A hand on my shoulder snapped me out of my sudden anger. I craned my neck to look at the offender, only to see that it was Ra. I was seething with anger at the thought of another war. I knew we would win it without hesitation-- but Iris. How would she fare against this army?

"You see, Seth, even though I'm not who I thought I was, I always have a plan in place. I should kill myself, because I am not as pure as I had hoped." Ian lowered his head in shame. "No matter. This world is going to die one way or another. If I get to die, so do all of you!" he scoffed as he hung his head, his blood-drenched hair sticking to his face.

Ra pulled me away from Ian with a firm tug on my shoulder. "Seth, I don't know if your temple is safe. Bring everyone here to the

Dome. It will keep them alive long enough for us to finish this once and for all," he whispered.

I placed a hand on my hip and let out a long breath. Pinching the bridge of my nose, I weighed the options. "Where's the book? We need to get it to Portú. He needs to finish the preparations on the land that's currently cleared. A few countries will just have to make do with what they have once everything is finished," I suggested.

Ra ran his hand through his hair, nodding as he turned and strode away from me. "Guess it's time to awaken the elemental, then."

A sudden tug at my heartstrings caused me to turn around. To my surprise, Iris was standing in the doorway. Two strands of her hair fell on each shoulder, framing her round face, which she wore in a half up, half down hairstyle. Her hands anxiously fiddled with the silk fabric of a golden, loose-fitting gown that hugged her chest. My jaw hit the floor at the power radiating from her.

I quickly walked over to her, grabbing her hand. "What are you doing up? You need to rest." I spoke with a softened tone.

Iris' eyes slowly raised to meet my gaze. I saw a blue, red, green, and white orb sat in alignment imbedded in her skin from her forehead to her chin. Her sapphire eyes glowed. "I don't know what's going on, but all of the commotion outside of the Dome... I couldn't sleep. Those things. They need to be killed, quickly."

I watched as single tears spilled from the corners of her beautiful eyes. I leaned down and kissed her forehead. "Don't worry about that. I'll take care of that. But right now, you need to head up to the mountain. I'll have Portú meet you there." I brought my hand to her cheek, wiping the tear with my thumb.

"But why? Are we starting the revival soon? What's going on, Seth? I need to know!" she shouted, causing the building to shake. The ground rumbled beneath our feet.

I plugged my ears with my fingers and sucked in a breath at the high-pitched ringing caused by Iris's voice. "Could you stop shouting?"

A force of wind hit me hard as Iris waved her hand, sending me flying across the room and crash landing on Atlas with a loud thud.

"Will you stop pissing her off?" Atlas grumbled as he shoved me off of him, rising to his feet.

"I'm not trying to piss her off. But every time she shouts, screams, or raises her voice to a certain pitch, the fucking world shakes, if you haven't noticed," I groaned, pushing myself up from the floor. I glanced over at Ra, who had a grin plastered across his face.

Ra chuckled as he shuffled over to Iris, taking her hands in his. "Come, I'll show you the world this monster has created. It's almost time."

A burst of bright light appeared around them as they disappeared. I clenched my fist and turned to Ian, who sat staring at the now empty space Iris and Ra had been standing in moments ago with sullen eyes. "She's not going to make it. She's not going to make it in time," he repeated. "The world will fall to its knees!" he laughed maniacally.

A growl erupted from my chest as I shifted into my true form and stared down at him. "This time, Ian, you're not coming back," I sneered.

"You can't kill him! He will just reincarnate again and do this all over again on another planet!" Atlas shouted.

"Oh, but I can keep his soul trapped in the underworld. He won't be given the opportunity to come back," I replied and reached out and grabbed him by his throat. My eyes fixated on his while I concentrated on his soul.

Ian's body shook, his yellow eyes dilated as he stared into my own. I smirked, merely pulling his soul from his ragged body, which fell limp against his shackles.

"You will never harm anyone else again," I sneered at him and I opened a portal to the underworld. Arms of the undead reached through and grabbed his soul and began to pull him down. Ian fought for his life. He kicked and screamed, shouted and cried out, begging not to go. "Send him to the labyrinth," I commanded and turned to Atlas, whose mouth was agape.

"Y-you just-- I mean I've never actually seen this happen before. That's uh, new..." he stumbled over his words.

I shrugged. "It's an 'every once in a while' sort of thing."

"You're just so nonchalant about it all. No wonder you--"

I snarled at Atlas. "Don't you fucking dare." I turned to leave and headed straight for the doors. "C'mon, we have work to do."

By the time we made it outside, the screams and cries of the human clones were easily penetrating through its walls. I glanced at Atlas, who wore the same dumbfounded look as I had before I enlarged my frame and charged off toward the horde.

Rage surged through me as I watched the walls of the dome crack, compromising the safety of those inside. I frantically searched for Iris.

Where are you? Honestly, I know Ra took you to the mountain, but I need your help down here.

I'm not too far away. I'm to the north.

I need you to put a wall around the Dome. These things are getting ready to break through.

I'm already on it. I can see it from here.

I let out a sigh of relief as I stopped at the edge. I slammed my fist into the ground and summoned my army. We needed all the help we could get at that moment.

Flocks of Avians appeared in the sky while my army rushed towards these hordes, pushing them away from the walls of the Dome. I stepped through the barrier and began clawing and stomping on the clones. I grabbed a man nearby and crushed him, letting out a fierce roar.

The screams and cries of these clones rang in my ears. I pivoted around and watched in awe as Iris and Ra stood upon a cloud. Her arms were raised in the air and her eyes were closed. The green orb on her chin glowed, and a wall of stone formed around the fractured shield, concealing it.

My heart swelled at her ability to put others before herself. I shifted my gaze back toward the hordes and growled and I continued smashing these beings into the ground. Pools of blood stained the soil, the trees, and my soldiers as they tore these clones apart one by one.

A high-pitched screech sounded from above, causing me to freeze in my steps and look to the sky. That sound was coming from Iris.

"Oh, fuck, here we go!" Atlas shouted from above.

The ground rumbled and shook as giant chasms cracked and crumbled open under the larger crowds of the clones, swallowing them with ease. I wasn't concerned for my army, but I was concerned for Iris's wellbeing. How much energy was she willing to use? I swallowed hard and kept my footing amidst the shaking of the Earth.

"Iris, that's enough!" I shouted at her. "We can't afford to fracture the surface any more than we already have!"

Iris stopped and glanced down at me with tired eyes. "I'm sorry. I just thought--"

"Don't apologize. Just conserve your energy for now. You've done more than enough!" I turned back to the corpse-ridden battlefield to continue slaughtering the remaining clones.

Chapter 22: Mind, Body and Soul

Iris

Watching from above the battlefield, I felt an overwhelming feeling of unjust anger which quickly shifted to dread, fear, and sorrow, wash over me. I couldn't stand by and do nothing. I turned to Ra with tearful eyes.

"Why would someone do something so cruel?"

Ra let out a heavy sigh and placed his hand on my shoulder. "It's because of people's hunger for power and greed. None of this was necessary or needed but was caused by a want. Now you understand the difference between the two." He smiled softly and turned his head to the opposing clouds. "Looks like the cavalry has decided to come. Late, but nevertheless, they are here."

I turned to look in the direction he was looking and watched as Asherah walked down from steps that formed in the clouds, accompanied by a few others I did not recognize. "Who is with Asherah?" I asked in a hushed tone.

"Just a few who decided that Earth was worth fighting for," he whispered in my ear as he maneuvered around me to greet them. "Asherah, I see you brought the cavalry. Isis, Horus, Geb." Ra slightly bowed his head as he greeted each of them.

My jaw hit the floor when he mentioned Isis. I remembered murdering Osiris, and I no longer felt an inch of guilt over it at all. My body worked against me as I approached them with my head held high. I folded my hands over each other gracefully in front of me.

The God named Horus scoffed when his eyes landed on me. "So, this is who everyone is making a fuss over, huh?" His muscles tensed while his sky blue eyes narrowed at me. He stood shirtless with a golden deshret crown upon his falcon head to symbolize that he was not the son of Isis.

I raised a brow, cocking my head. "You're one to talk. If you had done your job sooner, I wouldn't have had to come. Now, it's my responsibility to clean up this mess," I retorted.

Geb held his stomach as he let out a boisterous laugh. "Oh my. My son sure picked a feisty one."

What? Son? I screamed internally. "Did you just say--"

"Aren't you the maiden that murdered Osiris?" Isis cut me off, her arm crossed over her chest as she tapped her chin with her finger.

I nodded. "I did, because I had no choice. We pulled his limbs apart, and I have his head around here somewhere." I straightened my posture, then shrugged.

She pinched the bridge of her nose and shook her head. "Where did you leave his body?" She hissed, taking a step toward me, only to be stopped by Horus.

"It's not worth it," he mumbled, turning away. Isis pushed past him and jumped down from the skies.

I watched as her tiny figure stomped up to Seth and tapped on his leg. He ignored her for a moment, but then shifted his gaze to the clouds and folded his ears back when his eyes landed on his father.

Geb gave him a nod and hopped down from the cloud, also enlarging his frame to match Seth's. The two stared at one another with

Isis standing between the two. I watched in anticipation, as I had no clue of the history between them.

"Good luck finding him," I shouted sarcastically and turned back to the others. The horrified look on Horus' face caused me to chuckle.

"What? He didn't leave me many options to rid myself of his presence." I rolled my eyes and shuffled over to Asherah, who could not keep her hilarity at the situation from showing on h er face.

"Oh, my child, you are one of a kind indeed." She chuckled, placing a hand on my shoulder as she guided me over to another cloud, pointing over to the top of a mountain off in the distance that stood slightly taller than the others. "You need to be up there. That is Mount Everest. Portú is waiting for you."

I gave her a curt nod as she walked back to the others who had joined in on the battle below. "How are there still so many clones?" I whispered, glancing down at all of them.

Taking in a deep breath, I shifted my gaze back to the top of Everest. "Well, here goes nothing." I exhaled slowly and moved my feet as quickly as my damned dress would allow.

"So much stupid fabric. Why does this thing have to be so damn long!" I pouted, grabbing the bottom of the dress so I could continue on with my journey.

The sun began to set on the horizon. We were losing daylight quickly. My thoughts ran cold, as I hadn't contacted Seth in over six hours, nor had he tried to contact me. Was it because I was too far away? A soul tie shouldn't require a specific distance. Maybe? Ugh, this entire journey was causing my feet to ache. Even walking on clouds could become tiresome.

Seth? Where are you? Is everything okay? I'm worried.

Everything down here is handled. You keep going.

How many more are there?

Not too many, but I'll catch up with you soon. If you're tired, sit and wait for me. I'll carry you the rest of the way.

Okay, I'll do that. My feet are killing me, and I miss you.

I know. Just hang on. I'll be there soon.

I smiled to myself and knelt onto the plush cloud. My legs and hips ached. I placed my hands on the cloud to keep myself upright when a sharp pain stabbed at my chest. My breath was stolen in the wind. A blue light shined above me, causing me to look up to find that there was nothing there, but I could still see it. *What is this?*

Reaching up to my forehead, I felt a smooth lump and then another and another as I ran my hand from my forehead to my chin. I counted four in all. My eyes widened.

Ra, what is this on my face? Why didn't you tell me?

Did you not see them when you dressed?

I didn't... but--

Each orb symbolizes one of your elemental abilities.

Oh...

I let out a harsh breath and shook my head while watching the sunset. I was afraid Cyrus had perished amongst the clones, but it was not Cyrus's howl that changed the day to night, but Lupin's.

Why are people so selfish in their own actions? I wondered. *Maybe I should carry on. I need to get up to the top of that mountain and finish this once and for all.* I took my sweet time rising from the cloud and headed toward Everest at a very slow and painful pace.

"I thought I told you to wait for me," Seth grumbled from behind, causing me to turn around. I scanned him from head to toe. He was drenched in the blood of the fallen.

Smiling, I opened my arms to him and motioned for him to embrace me. "Come here."

"I wouldn't want you to get dirty." He took a cautious step towards me. His ears twitched.

I gave him the best puppy dog look I could muster up in my weakened state and motioned him forward. "Please?" I begged. Seth finally gave in and approached me.

He lifted me into his arms, cradling me, and kissed the top of my forehead. "Only because you said please." He chuckled lightheartedly. "Now, let's get you where you need to be."

I melted into him and rested my head against his bare chest, not caring about the smell of iron as we made our way to the top of the mountain.

"Why don't we just use one of your portals?" I asked, gazing up at him.

I could see his canine-like smirk, though he continued looking straight ahead. "Because I want to spend what little time we have left together."

What does that mean? Was Seth serious about me dying?

Seth and I spent our final moments together as we approached the meeting spot with Portú. His face remained hidden from me under the hood of his robe and his hands were clasped around the obsidian Book of Death. I pushed out every thought of death and fear from my mind as a familiar feeling washed over me. A voice in the back of my mind gave me the instructions. The voice was soothing yet frightening at the same time.

Little one, are you ready?

Ready for what?

You'll see. But, darling, please be calm and relaxed.

When you say it like that, it makes me want to do the opposite.

I know, my dear. Just breathe; you can do this. Your instructions are arriving as we speak.

My instruct-- "Woah!" I squeaked as a wave of energy surged through me. My energy levels were rejuvenated in a heartbeat, power flooding every fiber of my being. I had never felt so... alive.

I turned to Seth with raised eyebrows and bright eyes. "What just happened?"

Seth smiled and reached down to stroke my cheek. "It's time." He set me down gently, moved his hand to my lower back, and ushered me over to where Portú stood patiently waiting.

"Are you ready?" he hissed in a low tone.

I turned my gaze to Portú and nodded before turning back to Seth, my eyes watering. "I don't know if I can do this alone," I whispered. "Will you stay?" I asked.

Seth leaned down and kissed the top of my head once again. Using his hand, he tilted my chin up and pressed his lips against mine. The warmth of his lips brought joy and happiness for a moment before he pulled away.

I let out a long breath and turned to face the deserted land filled with ash below me. This seemed familiar but-- oh no. *This is the field... after the revival.*

I swallowed hard and let the energy flow through me, whatever the source. The shuffling of rocks rumbled behind me, and I turned my head slightly to see Seth down on one knee, bowing his head, his ears lowered. He, too, was chanting something I was unable to hear.

"Focus, child." Portú grumbled as he opened the book of the dead and began reading the scripture.

My head was forcefully pulled toward the sky as the words that were not my own spilled from my lips. My eyes stared into nothingness. The dark clouds that hovered overhead threatened to release another wave of deadly toxins into the atmosphere.

"*Mn aela riah alsama.*" The wind around us picked up, gathering the clouds into a hurricane that formed before us. I chanted the words over and over again, the tone of my voice ascending into a shout.

The white orb on the tip of my chin shined brightly and fell onto the soil. Moments later, I watched the light fade. It slowly absorbed into the ground, causing the Earth to rumble.

I smiled and continued on, feeling a part of my soul disappear into the Earth. *"Binar altabiea,"* I began chanting. The fire that fueled my soul ignited. The massive hurricane became enveloped in flames, as did the surface of the remainder of the world. The red orb on my forehead dropped and absorbed into the Earth, pulling another piece of me with it.

I stumbled as my energy drained. I coughed, the smell of iron invading my nose, brought my hand to my lips, and wiped it away to reveal that yes, this blood was my own.

I ignored every screaming fiber of my being and continued. *"La'aemaq 'aemaq albahr,"* I shouted as loud as I could. As I turned my eyes to the black ocean, its calm waves receded, then built into a wave as tall as the mountain. Rushing toward the shore, it washed away the hurricane, extinguishing the flames that had overtaken the land. It filled the land with smoke as the wave slowly receded back to the ocean whence it had arisen.

The blue orb shined bright and dropped from my forehead and onto the surface. It ripped yet another piece of my soul with it, causing me to fall to my knees. I let out a small cry and slammed my hands onto the Earth. I let out a heavy sigh and my hair came undone, falling beside me. Blood seeped from my lips while I attempted to catch my breath and tears fell from my eyes when I looked to what was left of the Earth before me.

"Just, one… more," I panted. Pushing myself up from the ground, I raised my arms to the side, palms up, and used the last of my energy to shout the final incantation of the ritual.

"Tamat aistieadat al'ard al'umi!" As the words left my lips, the green orb shined bright and did as the others had done before them. It fell from right under my bottom lip onto the Earth and receded.

I let out a weakened cry of joy as the surface of the Earth shined green and began sprouting all sorts of life-- from lush green grass to all of the rare and exotic trees. The nearby streams flowed with crystal-clear water. Even extinct wildlife rose from the ground and ran to their hearts' content. The world was restored to her natural glory.

My heart throbbed with love and joy as I weakly spun around to face Seth. I could feel the last bit of my soul pull away from me like an invisible web. Extending my hand to him, my weakened body crumbled to the ground with a heavy thud.

I could hear Seth calling out to me when he came into view. His mouth continued to move, but I could not hear what he was saying. My eyes became heavy. I couldn't help but smile when I whispered my final words to him. "My love. We did it."

I was pulled into a blanket of warmth as the darkness engulfed me.

Screams and cries of the souls invaded my ears. My body writhed in pain, and I rolled onto my side, slowly opening my eyes I gazed around in search of a familiar view. "Where am I now?" I groaned.

The ground below me was cold, and the open space was filled with grey clouds and dimmed lights from an infinite burning torch. The wandering souls of those who had lost their way and those who had not been judged favorably.

"Where else do you think the dead go?" an ethereal voice growled at me.

My head shot up as my eyes landed on a familiar figure. His darkened skin and tall pointed ears resembled Seth's figure, except this God in front of me was bit shorter. I clenched my fist and let out a harsh breath. "You must be Anubis, and that tells me I ended up exactly where I was hoping I wouldn't."

"Well, what did you expect when you gave your life to revive the surface? Such a naive girl to think you'd be able to survive that." He smirked, extending his hand to me. "Come we must get going. If your soul lingers here too long, you will become one of them, and that is not the goal here."

I batted his hand away and pushed myself from the ground slowly, wincing with every move I made. "So, I really am dead." Sadness and despair washed over me as I rose to my feet. My eyes watered. "May I ask a favor?" I asked, shifting my gaze up at him.

"What is it you need, child?" he growled. His grip on his staff tightened as he visibly become impatient.

I swallowed hard. "Could you send a message to Seth? Please, I beg you."

Anubis huffed and faded into a cloud of smoke. I awaited an answer only to be pushed onto the path by another force. "Let's go, Iris. You've done enough." A feminine voice said from beside me.

I turned my head to glance back at the pathway, hoping Anubis would show up before I got too far along. "Why isn't he coming? Shouldn't he know that I'm here? Protector of the undead but he has no idea that I'm here." I sniffled as my eyes began to water.

The feminine voice sighed. "I am sorry, Iris. But things aren't always what they seem. You were never supposed to end up here. Not like this."

I stopped dead in my tracks and turned to the woman. I had no idea who she was, and I had not seen her before. "W-who are you?"

She gave me a sad smile. "I am Anput, wife to Anubis and I am here to guide you to the scales."

Lowering my head, I closed my eyes and rolled my bottom lip inward to hold back my tears. "Can we just wait—"

"Iris, don't think that you're special because you won the heart of the God of chaos. He is just that--the monster he truly is. The God of tricks and deception. Do you really think he loves you?" a soldier sneered.

Those words cut through me like a knife. What did he mean by that? I knew deep down inside what this man was saying was all lies. But I couldn't help but wonder if he was right. I silently prayed to Seth, but when he didn't show, my heart sank in my chest. I had only hoped at that point that my heart would have what the scales needed. "Don't you forget about me, Seth."

Anput laid her hand on my shoulder. "My dear, ignore them. He does love you. Just wait and see."

Chapter 23: Wandering Soul

Seth

I sat atop the mountain, Iris's limp body in my arms. My heart and soul fell into oblivion as tears continually streamed down my fur. I had hoped and even prayed that this wouldn't happen. I thought she was stronger than this.

My lip quivered as I ran my fingers through her hair. I couldn't let the world see me, Seth, God of the underworld, chaos and trickery, crying over a woman.

I perked my ears as I turned my gaze from Iris to the fields before us. The lush green grass, lush trees, and crystal-clear streams. Even the wildlife had returned. The revival ritual was a success, but in return, Mother God took her from me. A sacrifice. The one thing I always hated about being a God was the simple fact that we could, and most likely would, outlive our loved ones.

"You did it, love. You did it," I whispered as I choked back tears. I cradled her body and pressed my forehead to hers.

"I will never love another woman, ever. You will be my last." I sniffled, rising to my feet, my hold on Iris unwavering, I turned to the sky, shouting at the top of my lungs. "Are you fucking happy now? Huh? Are you fucking satisfied? Asherah! Answer me!"

"You told her what was going to happen. You weighed the options, just as the scale does in the afterlife. Don't act like this is my fault. Iris will not have wasted her life in vain." Asherah's voice invaded my ears.

"You." I turned around, clutching Iris's body. "You set me up to love another, just to have her die? You..." A sharp pain stabbed at my heart. "You really believe I am not worthy of anything but pain and misery. Then, so be it," I growled.

I opened a portal to my temple just outside of King Tutankhamun's pyramid and stood in silence as I scanned the area. Dust had settled upon my altar, furniture, and other personal effects.

I stalked over to a small casket I'd had my disciples make for any occasion, not realizing it was going to be for my beloved. I knelt, pushed the solid obsidian lid open, and gently laid Iris onto the plush Egyptian cotton mat. I leaned down to kiss her forehead and stroke her cheek with my thumb. "Sleep well, little one. May we meet again," I whispered before closing the lid.

I rose and ran my hand through my fur. Needing something to occupy my mind, I scoffed, and a low rumble escaped my lips. "This place is a fucking mess," I growled.

Opening a portal to the underworld, I summoned a few of Anubis' soldiers to clean the place up while I sat on my throne. Memories of Iris swirled through my mind as my soldiers began lighting candles, bringing life to my shrine.

Gold and stone statues filled the place with offerings previously laid by the villages for their loved ones as they passed through the gates to the scales. Most didn't know that their hearts would be weighed against the feathers of Ma'at. I couldn't bear to look at it; my gaze instead locking onto Iris's casket.

I sat and thought of the memories of my little love. From her high cheek bones to her little nose. Her bright sapphire eyes that danced with life.

Hey, could you toss me up there? Iris's voice echoed in my head.

Hey, you did that on purpose! The memory of my little flustered Iris made me chuckle.

I love you, too.

I stared for Ra-knows-how-long. My pounding, aching heart pulled me in her direction, but I chose to ignore the feeling.

I noticed Anubis in my peripheral view as he approached me. His golden chest plate reflected a beam of light from one of the lit torches just below my feet. "Seth, there's a mortal who is requesting you by name," he grumbled, annoyed.

I raised my head, a brow arched. I couldn't think of anyone who would want to see me. I shook my head and dismissed him. "I am not in the mood to meet with anyone."

"Do you truly not know where your love went?" he smirked before turning to walk away.

I thought for a moment and rubbed my chin. "Wait, what? How long has it been since the revival?" I asked.

He stopped and turned his head in my direction with a sickening crack. "Seven days. She's been asking for you for quite some time. The elemental, right?" He tapped his chin.

"Shit!" I jumped to my feet and dropped into a portal, appearing at the end of the line to the scales. My eyes scanned the heads of the other lost souls, eventually landing on the snow-white tresses of my one and only.

I pushed through the crowd toward the front of the line. My heart throbbed and anxiety coursed through me. "Iris…" My voice was low. I could see her shoulders relax as she turned around to face me. My eyes widened at the sight, and a smile formed on my lips.

Her eyes were filled with tears, and a sad smile was painted on her face. She then took hesitant steps towards me. "Seth!" she cried. "I didn't think you'd actually show!"

"If I had known your soul was going to stay here in this timeline, I would have brought you back myself. You wouldn't have come here." I extended my hand to her.

The loud bang of a staff hitting the ground echoed through the labyrinth. I craned my neck at the soldier who stood stoic, just as I had made him, and narrowed my eyes before turning back to Iris.

"Seth, you know the rules," the soldier's voice sounded from behind me.

I shifted my ear in his direction and growled. "I created the rules, and this one, I'm willing to break them for. She's coming with me," I shouted at him.

"Seth, you won't be taking that one anywhere," he threatened as he widened his stance, the tip of his spear pointed at me.

"Little one, give me a moment." I kissed the top of her head and turned to face the soldier. I bared my teeth and snarled at him. "Once alive, now in death. You shall face your demise with the scales. A soldier no more," I grumbled and stomped my foot, the ground below him crumbling when a hole appeared. His flesh turned to ashes as he fell apart, falling into the pit.

The gasps of those witnessing the event quickly turned to whispers amongst themselves.

Ignoring the onlookers, I turned to face Iris, only to lock eyes with Anubis standing behind the crowd. He gave me a simple nod of approval and slowly faded into the darkness.

Once he was out of sight, I shifted my attention back to Iris and extended my hand to her. "Come."

Iris placed her small hand in mine, and I pulled her closer to me. Leaning down, I inhaled her scent and curled my fingers through her snow-white tresses. I stood in disbelief that she was actually here with me again.

Gently pulling her arm, I held her close as I walked back toward the end of the line and dropped into a portal back to my temple.

I wrapped my arms around her and held her tightly but then realized I was holding her soul and not her physical body. Turning to the casket, I threw open the lid and looked down only to see that it indeed was empty.

"What the hell?" I turned back to Iris, who was taking a deep breath.

"Oh, I missed my body so!" She smiled at me as a bright light faded from behind her. The color of her skin returned, and her sapphire eyes swirled with life.

Asherah, what is the meaning of this?

Being a god, I thought you knew of The Great Sacrifice.

How could I have not remembered this?

You seem to be forgetting a lot more these days. She's now the Elemental Goddess. Treat her well.

I stood with my jaw on the floor as Iris took a hesitant step toward me. Her eyes were filled with worry.

"Seth, is something wrong?" Iris asked, her fingers fiddling with the hem of her gown.

I quickly picked her up and hugged her as tight as I could without hurting her. "Iris, you don't understand how—"

"—sad, lonely, depressed you were?" she finished after me. Iris wrapped her arms around my neck and squeezed just as hard. "You have no idea how scared I was. I didn't want to leave and then... my escort reminded me that we won the war. Everyone there knew who I was, so I requested to have you come. I had been asking for you for days, but you never came..."

A wave of sadness washed over me. My ears flattened against my head as I lowered my gaze. "I didn't get your message until a few hours ago. I--I'm sorry."

"Don't apologize! You still managed to get to me before the scales were weighed. I'm just happy you showed." She nuzzled her face into the crook of my neck.

I pulled away for a moment, shifting back into my human form, and gazed into her sapphire eyes. It was in this moment I knew I wanted her to be mine, more than just a soul tie, but something that meant more to her as well.

"Iris... Will you marry me?" I asked with confidence.

Iris's breath was caught in her throat. She froze for a moment, pulling away to face me before giving me an answer.

"Seth, I would want nothing more than to be your wife. For eternity."

THE END.

Bonus Scene

The sweet scent of her arousal awakened me from a deep sleep. Her back was flushed against my skin as we laid entangled in one another. I pulled my leg from between hers earning me a series of cute sleepy moans as she rolled onto her stomach, tucking her head into the pillow.

I couldn't help but smile watching Iris sleep. She was adorable and sexy, yet fierce. It had been a few months since the revival ritual had taken place and we've spent every waking moment together and even planned our little human-like wedding ceremony.

My eyes scanned over her naked figure beneath the sheets. I could feel my cock throb as I began salivating. I needed to taste and feel every inch of her.

I shouldn't wake her. She needs the rest. I thought. But my cock said otherwise as it twitched. Precum oozed from the tip saturating the sheet that concealed it.

Fuck it...

I propped myself behind her as I pulled the sheet off, the view of her plump ass pushed me over the edge. Spreading her legs, I lowered myself to her entrance and leaned down into the crook of her neck "Little one." I whispered huskily in her ear "It's time to wake up!" With that I rammed my cock into her from tip to base.

Iris's head jolted up as she screamed. I could see her hands shift under the pillow as she arched her back, pushing against me. "Seth!" She screamed.

"Yes my love? You want more?" I growled seductively in her ear. "I can fuck you all morning if you want. My cock has been craving you." I gave her a teasing thrust.

Iris squeaked and squirmed beneath me. "Mmm, yes please." She purred, arching her head toward me. Her sapphire eyes stared back at me with pure lust. Biting her lip she pushed her ass into my crotch, beckoning me for more.

I gripped her waist and kissed her lips as I began thrusting my cock into her. Iris's ass bounced against me. Her moans grew louder as she lowered herself to the bed, her legs spread wide for me. I pulled back and reached between her legs and began rubbing her clit in gentle circles.

I could feel her pussy tighten around me. Before she could cum, I pulled out, flipped her onto her back and positioned my head between her legs. Oh, the sweetest aroma invaded my senses. Using my fingers, I spread her pussy open and took a moment to appreciate its perfection.

Iris's legs shifted beside my head, her hands gripped my hair, "That's not fair. You can't just fuck the shit out of me, stop before I can cum and just... ugh." She whined.

I chuckled and ran my tongue along the outline of her entrance before making my way to her clit. Its soft bud stuck out ever so slightly as I massaged it. Moving myself down I penetrated her pussy with my tongue. Her sweet juices gushed, soaking my chin and face.

Her thighs squeezed my head as her hips bucked and ground against my face. Her body trembled as I inserted two fingers into her pussy and rubbed her clit with my thumb. I loved the way she sounded, her singing of moans and the way she squirmed.

"I can do what I want, little love. And there's nothing you can do about it besides submit to me." I said with a husky tone. Pulling away from her i continued to finger fuck her as I brought my lips to hers, giving her a taste of her own juices turned me on even more than I could imagine. The way she ran her tongue over my skin to get every drop of her juices from me earned her an ethereal growl.

Iris gently bit my lip and tugged as her breath hitched and her body began to convulse. I wrapped my arm around her so she couldn't escape this pleasure. "That's it. Ride that out."

Her panting became frantic as she clawed at my arms. "Seth, please. Stop… Stop! Oh! It's too much!"

Leaning down I bit her neck and whispered into her ear, "No, I'm not stopping until I get every last drop of cum out of you." I pulled my soaked fingers from her pussy and ram my cock back into her. Her walls spasmed and tightened around me. Massaging her insides with every thick inch I had.

I lifted her into my arms, forcing her to straddle me. With one hand I gripped her waist and forced my cock deeper into her with each thrust.

"Seth, y-you're going to rip me apart!" She stumbled over her words as she rode out another orgasm.

I slowed my thrusts and held her close as her body fell limp.

"Done so soon?" I teased, stopping my thrusts.

"Oh, you're evil." She playfully scowled at me as she rested her head against my chest, breathing heavily.

I ran my free hand down her back ever so lightly. I chuckled as she twitched and squirmed, giggling in response.

I shifted my legs from underneath me and fell backward onto the bed. Iris squeaked as she fought to stay up.

"What was that for?" She whined, pushing herself to sit up.

I placed my hands on her hips and let out a long breath. "It's fun to watch you get all flustered. You're adorable." I smiled up at her.

Iris pouted at me and ground her hips into me, I flexed my cock inside of her and watched as she let out a low moan.

"Stop that!" She squealed.

"Or what?" I challenged back.

"Or—I'll— Grr." She growled at me. Iris placed her hands on my lower abdomen and began slowly sliding up and down on my shaft all while squeezing her walls around me.

I closed my eyes and placed my hands on her thighs as she slammed herself down on my cock. I grunted and moaned with her as she continued.

"Seth," She huffed. "I-I'm gonna cum again!" She screamed as she slammed herself down one last time, her walls twitched and gripped my cock like a vice as she came. My cock flexed inside of her and pumped her full of my seed as I let out a loud moan.

"Fuck! Iris! Why didn't you-"

Iris fell limp against my chest, huffing as our juices flowed out of her and onto me and all over the bed. "I, want... more" She panted. "I don't know what's wrong with me."

I rolled her from on top of me and flipped her onto her back to face me. "Is that fire inside growing, or did something awaken?" I asked, worried about my tone.

"I don't know. Seth I really don't know." She panted beneath me. Her hands roamed over her body as if something were crawling on her. I really began to worry for her.

Iris gripped the sides of her head and let out a horrifying screech. I braced myself and waited for the earth to shake as it always had but nothing came. "What the hell? Iris what's wrong?"

I wrapped my arms around her and pulled her into my lap. "Talk to me. What's happening?" I soothed, pressing her head against my chest. I knew she could hear my heartbeat.

"Asherah!" I shouted.

"My God you two what the— oh my goodness what happened to her?"

Iris's body slowly began to fade from my arms.

"Shit… She's gone back to her timeline."

Asherah inhaled a deeply, shaking her head. "Well, at least she will know the truth between your bond now."

Made in the USA
Las Vegas, NV
24 March 2022

46186599R00121